SWEAR TO ME

THE CLARKE BROTHERS: BOOK TWO

LILIAN MONROE

1

DOMINIC

I LOVE the smell of sulfur that hits my nose when the match bursts to life.

I watch the tiny flame for a second as it shifts and dances in the light breeze. I glance up at the sky, littered with a million stars, and then down to the huge, looming building in front of me.

I can smell the gasoline soaking into the ground and into the timber at my feet. The luxury hotel is like a stain on the side of the mountain. It shouldn't be here. Still, as I stand here with the match in my hand, I can't help but hesitate.

My brother Ethan drops his match. I hear the whoosh and crack of a new fire coming to life across the construction site. Sheriff Whittaker is next, igniting the north side of the building. I watch the two fires start to lick at the new construction. They climb up the bare beams and travel along the trails of gasoline that we sprayed all over the ground floor.

The match is burning close to my fingers. I watch the small flame for a second more, and finally drop it at my feet. I take a step back as the gasoline ignites. It starts as a low blue flame, traveling fast along the fuel that I just splashed over the ground. A deep sense of satisfaction wells up inside me as I watch the fire ignite. I'm transfixed, watching the flames as they dance along the side of the half-built hotel. The heat of the fire starts to warm my face and clothes until it's almost too much. When it starts climbing up the beams, I turn away and walk back toward the trailhead where we came from.

Ethan and Bill are already there. They nod at me, and the three of us turn toward the building once again. We watch it in silence until the flames have overtaken the half-constructed luxury hotel.

"Let's get out of here," Ethan says in a low voice. I grunt in response and turn back toward the trail. We walk in silence, waiting a few minutes before fishing our head lamps out of our pockets and turning them on. It's a two-mile hike before we get to the old logging road where we parked our trucks.

When we get there, Bill extends a hand toward me. "Good work, Dominic. Ethan. I never thought I'd commit a felony as Sheriff, but I can't feel guilty about this one. That hotel would have been the end of this town – and the end of these forests as we know them."

"It's better off gone," Ethan replies. Bill nods his hand and heads toward his truck. I jump into mine and Ethan gets into the passenger seat. The engine rumbles to life and the two of us head back down toward the town of Lang Creek.

We crest a hill and I see the fire burning behind us in my rear-view mirror. I stop the truck and jump out. Ethan follows. We climb into the bed of the pickup and watch the fire burn for a few minutes. As the flames lick higher and higher, the corners of my lips start to lift up with it. A siren wails in the distance, and Ethan and I exchange a knowing look.

Gradually, a laugh starts rolling through my chest until my shoulders are shaking and I'm throwing my head back. I clap my brother on the back and he grins at me.

"I can't believe we fucking did that," I finally say as I shake my head.

Ethan laughs. "I can."

"Let's go," I finally say, staring at the fire one last time and shaking

*my head. As we drive away, the smell of smoke lingers in my nostrils
and I grin. It's a crime, and it should be wrong, but it feels so, so right.*

ONE YEAR LATER...

I LOOK at the dregs of beer left in the bottom of my bottle and I
sigh. It's probably time to go home now. My brother Aiden and
his new wife Madeline are cuddling at the long table with stars in
their eyes.

It was a great ceremony and a beautiful wedding that the
whole town came to. I'm happy for him, of course. He's my
brother. How could I *not* be happy for him? He's found a beautiful
wife, started his own garage and hardware store in town, and
finally found happiness. After ten years of grief following Dad's
death, that's something to celebrate. I just can't shake the feeling
that something isn't right.

Maybe this sour feeling in the pit of my stomach is just plain
old jealousy.

I jump when Bill Whittaker puts his hand on my shoulder. He
hands me a new beer and I nod in thanks.

"Why the long face, Dominic? Aren't you happy for your
brother?"

"Delighted," I say. "Just tired, I think. Long day."

Bill takes a seat next to me. He spreads his legs wide and
sighs. It's strange seeing him in regular clothes. He's usually
wearing his dark blue uniform and wide-brim hat. Even when we
snuck through the forest to burn down that damned hotel, he
was in uniform. He looks over at Aiden and Maddy and nods.

"They make a good couple. Aiden deserves a bit of peace."

I don't bother looking over at my brother and his new wife. I
grunt in response and put my empty beer bottle down on the

table in front of me. The plastic chair groans underneath me as I move, and I wonder how long until it collapses. It probably wasn't made for someone my size.

Bill stares at me for a few moments. "Are you okay, Dominic? Ever since that whole thing with the hotel..."

"I'm fine," I interrupt. "Fine."

Bill stares at me and nods his head a few times. "Are you having regrets?"

"Regrets?" I say, shifting my weight again and looking at him. I snort, and for the first time in hours, my lips curl into a grin. "Not a fucking chance."

Bill laughs and raises his beer toward me. I clink my fresh bottle against his and smile again, shaking my head. "Best thing we ever did was burn that thing down," I say before taking a sip.

"Yup," Bill replies.

The two of us fall into a comfortable silence and I think about that night last year. The whole town was up in arms about the new luxury hotel being built on the outskirts of town. When it burned down, it was like everyone celebrated for weeks. Everyone except the McCoys, obviously. They owned part of the new hotel before it *unfortunately* went up in flames.

People suspected my brothers and me, and the three of us were treated like heroes. Aiden didn't have anything to do with it, but it's not the type of thing you talk about after it's done. I hadn't expected that much attention. They still look at me differently, even a year later. It's almost like a sort of reverence.

The McCoys haven't said a word to me since the whole thing happened, and I'm not complaining. They keep to their side of town, and I keep to mine. I still have that deep, endless desire to get even with them, but I don't know how.

I shake my head to pull myself out of my reverie and nod to Bill.

"I'll see you around, Bill. Time for me to head home."

"Take it easy, big fella."

I stand up and stretch my body. I've been working hard at my workshop lately, and every muscle in my body is screaming for rest.

"Hey," Bill calls out as I turn away. I look over my shoulder at him. "You heard Mara McCoy's coming back?"

I frown as I think of the McCoy girl. I shake my head. "No, is she?"

"Due back any day now. Didn't work out with her rich businessman."

I grunt in response before turning away. Why is he telling me that? Why would I care? Something stirs in the depth of my stomach as I think of the McCoy girl, but I shake my head and ignore it.

It takes a few minutes to say my goodbyes, and I breathe a sigh of relief when I finally head down the mountain toward my little cabin on the outskirts of town.

As much as I love my brother, and as much as I'm happy for him, I can't wait to be back in the peace and quiet of my own four walls.

2

MARA

"THE CAR IS WAITING OUTSIDE, MA'AM," Claire says. I look at my fiancé's personal assistant and nod. Well, *ex*-fiancé's personal assistant, I guess.

I zip up my last suitcase and stand it up. Claire makes a move toward me, but I hold up a hand.

"It's okay, I'll bring it down."

"Sure," she says. She's a true professional. This whole time, she's kept a straight face and helped me as much as she could as I moved out of this beautiful house. I've called this place home for the past two years, and now I'm being thrown out like some kind of squatter. Vincent didn't even have the decency to come here himself. He sent his assistant to deal with me, and that stings almost as much as the breakup.

I swallow my bitterness and square my shoulders. Lifting my chin up, I wheel the last of my suitcases out the door. I hear it click shut behind me and Claire's footsteps follow a few seconds later. We walk down the hallway in silence, both staring straight ahead. Not a word is spoken between us until we walk out the front door and get to the car. The driver grabs my suitcase from

6

me and packs it into the trunk before opening the back door for me.

I have one foot already in the car when Claire clears her throat. I look at her, wondering what other ridiculous request Vincent has made. I almost feel sorry for her. *She* still has to put up with him.

"Miss McCoy," she says, hesitating. "For what it's worth, I thought you were wonderful. I'm sorry –"

"Don't apologize, Claire," I say as a pang passes through my heart. "It's not you that should be sorry. And for the last time, call me Mara!"

There's a hint of a grin on Claire's face, and she nods her chin down once. "Mara, then. Good luck."

I climb into the car as the driver shuts the door. He slides into the driver's seat and thankfully doesn't say a word to me as we head toward the airport. We drive through the winding roads, packed with mansion after mansion before we get onto the freeway. I watch the buildings go by and bid a silent goodbye to Silicon Valley.

Maybe this is for the best. I'm not a California girl. Never was, and probably never will be. I've never fit in here. I'm from a tiny town in the heart of the Adirondack mountains, where the trees are old and the mountains are older. I take a deep breath and close my eyes, leaning my head back on the headrest.

A tear falls from the corner of my eye and I quickly brush it away. I didn't think it would end this way, and the shock of it still hurts almost more than the fact that it's over. Like a fool, I thought Vincent actually loved me. I thought he'd wanted to spend the rest of his life with me. Like a fool, I thought the construction of the hotel at Lang Creek was secondary to our relationship. I thought that luxury hotel brought us together, and *love* united us – not the money the hotel would bring.

I was wrong.

It stings – the rejection. It makes my heart squeeze and my cheeks burn when I think about it. How could I be so stupid? I should have known at the very beginning. I saw Vincent's demeanor change from cold and distant to charming the instant the hotel deal was on the table. I should have known it wasn't love.

I was nothing but a pawn that my parents used. *Again.*

Another tear escapes my eyes and I brush it away angrily. I set my jaw. I'm not going to let that happen again. I won't be used and sold off to some rich businessman just so my parents can profit off it.

That hotel burning down was the best thing that ever happened to me. Now I know who Vincent is, and I won't be married to him for the rest of my life. Now I know that my parents think they can use me for their own personal gain.

The bitterness seeps into my veins and I savor the taste of it. I've been such a fool. I've believed I was loved and appreciated for who I was, but I've only ever been loved for what I have. And now? What do I have? A broken engagement, no money, no prospects... I've got nothing. I have to go back to the people that put me in this position in the first place.

My parents got a tidy sum from the insurance company when the hotel burned down. That helped ease their fury at the whole thing. They still haven't forgiven the Clarke brothers, but what can they do when the Sheriff himself won't do anything about it?

I smile as I think of the small-town politics I'm about to fly back into. It's like a hornet's nest, and for the first time in my life I'm going back with my eyes wide open. I know who my parents are. I know how they've built their business and made their money, and I know that it hasn't been from honest, hard work.

I don't want to be a part of that – but for now, I need some time to get back on my feet. I'm still reeling from Vincent breaking off the engagement, and my head spins whenever I think of my parents.

I just need some time to figure everything out. I need to figure out who *I* am and what *I* want. I won't be used in any other business deals. I won't be sold off to the highest bidder and then returned when it all falls to pieces. I'm going to go back home and tell them *exactly* what I think of them.

The driver pulls up to the airport departures and hops out of the driver's seat. By the time I've climbed out of the car, he's found a cart and started loading my bags onto it. He smiles at me sadly and touches his cap.

"Good luck, Miss McCoy."

"Thanks, Will. Take care."

I grab the handle on the cart and set off toward the airport's sliding glass doors without looking back. My heart is beating and my mouth feels dry as I check into my flight and make my way through security. I never thought I'd be this nervous to go home.

When the plane lifts off the runway, I watch the brown and green hills fall away beneath me. I catch a glimpse of the ocean before we turn east and I bid it another silent goodbye. My heart feels a little bit lighter when I think of the mountains I'm heading back to. My lips curl into a smile and I rest my head back in my seat. I close my eyes and take a deep breath. All I breathe is stale airplane air, but I can almost taste the sweet, fresh air of the Adirondack mountains. In a few short hours, I'll be home.

3

DOMINIC

I WAKE up to the grey light of dawn – to an aching body and a pounding headache. I didn't think I'd drank that much at the wedding, but maybe my age is finally catching up to me. I groan as I get out of bed and stretch my stiff limbs. There's a chill in the air, even though summer is on its way. A shiver passes through my body and I rub my eyes before getting up.

It's not until the scalding hot water from the shower hits my body that I truly start to wake up. I wash myself slowly until I can move normally again, and then pour myself some coffee before heading out to the workshop.

The mug is steaming and I can see my breath as I make the short walk across the yard toward my workshop. It's bigger than my house, but I don't mind. I don't need much room to live, but I do need room to work. I throw open the door and turn the space heater on to warm up the shop. I'll need my fingers to be working properly. I've got a lot of detail work to finish up today.

My father is the one who showed me the basics of woodworking. He bought me my first tools and encouraged me to make toys and small pieces of furniture from the time I was a pre-teen. Every time I walk into the workshop and smell the sawdust and fresh cut wood, it takes me back to my youth. I turn to my work-bench and look at the half-finished chair that's laying there. I'll have to finish the whole set by the end of the week to fill this order. After that, I'm not sure what I'll do. My list of orders is worryingly short.

Furniture-making suits me. I like being alone. I like working alone. The hum of the lathe and the whining of the saw never fails to clear my head and put me in a state of Zen. I grab the intricate latticework that I started on the back of the chair and inspect yesterday's work.

Not bad.

Business was growing, for a while. I was making a name for myself as the best custom furniture maker in the area. I was even starting to get orders from out of state. But when the hotel burned down, it suddenly seemed like a lot of the bigger compa-nies didn't want to be associated with me anymore.

I keep telling myself it was the right thing to do – that in the long run it's best that the hotel doesn't exist. Still, I wish it hadn't had such a dramatic effect on my business. I lost a couple contracts, and then things slowed so much that I'm starting to get worried about where my next job will come from.

It's not a good place to be. I glance over at the table and half-finished chairs that I've made for this order, and I try to ignore the gnawing thought at the back of my mind:

After this one, I've got nothing.

I take a sip of coffee and put the thought out of my mind. I take a piece of oak and measure it up for a chair leg. Soon, I'm in my element. I'm not thinking about the next job, or money, or my brother and his wife, or the hotel. I'm not thinking about Mara, or why I care that she's coming back. All that exists is the grain of the wood under my calloused fingers and the smell of sawdust in the workshop.

Soon, I'm taking off my jacket and turning off the space

heater. I brush my hair off my forehead and open the big garage door at the front of the workshop to let some cool air in.

The late spring sun is starting to warm up the earth, and I take a moment to breathe in the fresh mountain air. The cobwebs in my mind have cleared. I know things will work out – they always do. I'm just not sure how. At the end of the day, I'm working for myself in this little paradise in the Adirondacks. What else could I want?

As the thought crosses my mind, a truck turns down the quiet road leading to my home and stops out front of the workshop. Aiden and his new bride hop out.

"Dominic!" he calls out, raising his hand in the air.

I nod to them. "Aiden, Maddy," I say. It's the first thing I've said all morning, and the words come out as a growl.

"We wanted to stop by to say thank you for yesterday. Your speech was beautiful. Here," Maddy says, handing me a small box.

I shake my head. "You didn't need to get me anything," I say.

She smiles. "Open it."

I lift off the cover and pull out a thick frame around a small wooden figure of a bear. The corners of my mouth lift up and I start to chuckle.

"My first wood carving," I say, shaking my head. I look at the two of them. "Where did you find this?"

"Found a box of Dad's things in the attic," Aiden responds. "He kept it all those years. Maddy thought it would be nice to frame it for you."

I feel my chest get heavy, and a wave of guilt washes over me. I shouldn't have been jealous yesterday or gotten upset at them. Maddy has lifted Aiden's spirits and made him into a new man. He's laughed more in the past year than he did in the whole decade before it. She's always thinking of all three of us brothers. My eyes prickle, and I nod as I look at the carving.

"At least I've gotten better since then," I say with a grin. "Workmanship isn't the greatest."

"Dominic," Maddy chides with a laugh. "You were nine years old." She pauses and smiles at me. "Do you like it?"

"I love it," I say. This time my voice is choked with emotion, but I hide it with a cough. I look at the wall where I hang all my hand tools. Dad's old tools are in the place of honor in the middle of the wall. I walk over and put a hook in the pegboard, and then hang the framed carving beside Dad's favorite chisel. I take a step back as Aiden and Maddy appear at my side. Aiden puts his hand on my shoulder and nods.

"Looks good," he says.

I can only nod in response. I don't trust my voice. It *does* look good. I can't believe my father kept that stupid little bear all those years. I think of all the hours and days he spent teaching me the craft and I shake my head.

I need to keep this business going. If not for myself, then for his memory. I stare at the frame for a few more seconds before turning to my brother and Maddy.

"You guys heading off now?"

They look at each other and smile. "Yep," Maddy says. "Honeymoon, here we come!"

"Take care of yourself," Aiden says as he extends his hand to shake mine.

I grunt. "You keep saying that to me," I say. "Are you worried I won't?"

"Just take care of yourself. I'll see you in a couple weeks."

I watch them get back into their truck and drive off. A small cloud of dust follows their car down the gravel road, and I watch it until the pickup disappears around the corner. I turn back toward the pegboard and look at my first wood carving one more time. The memories that I've tried so hard to push aside start flooding in.

I think of the hours that my father spent with me. The patience he had. The encouragement he gave me. I stare at the bear for an eternity before shaking my head and looking at the chair on my workbench. All I can do is make this chair the best chair I've ever made. All I can do is try to do my best work and hope that people start noticing again.

4

———

MARA

"MARA! Let me help you with those bags!"

"Thanks, Mom," I say, hauling the last of my suitcases out of the car and onto the sidewalk. She wraps me in a hug and I can't help but feel like it's all an act.

I've played this moment over and over in my mind for the past two days. How should I react when I see her? What should I say to her?

I've thought of a thousand different monologues that I could say to my mother and father. I could tell them that I see them for what they are – that I don't appreciate being treated like a bargaining chip. I could tell them that breaking off the engagement with Vincent has torn me up inside. I could tell them I blame them for putting me in that position.

Now that I'm here, though, I don't know what to say. My mother's arms are around me and I stare at the town's hotel over her shoulder.

My childhood home.

My room was on the ground floor, all the way down at the back. I never wanted for anything. I got sent away for private schooling, but then decided to strike out on my own. I got a job and put myself through school and was able to get a degree as an interior designer. But then, my career got put on hold when I met Vincent. My parents didn't approve of my ambitions.

I shouldn't be mad at them, but I am.

I should be grateful for all they gave me, but all I can focus on is what they held back.

Their love.

I remember when Aiden Clarke and I were dating. He was my first boyfriend, and I was head over heels in love with him. It was practically an arranged marriage, the way our two families were aligned. I remember seeing the way his father looked at him – the way he'd ruffle his hair and put his arm around his kids. I remember the sharp pain in my heart when I'd see that, knowing that I'd never get it from my own family.

When Aiden's father died, I felt responsible. I *still* feel responsible. Based on his reaction last time I saw him, Aiden definitely still blames me for it. All three brothers do, I think. After all, it was *me* who fell in the river that day. It was *me* that Mr. Clarke jumped in to save. It was *my* fault he got pneumonia. At the end of the day, it was my fault he died.

My parents bought out the Clarke's trucking and transportation business to 'help pay for hospital bills.' Like a fool, I believed it. It wasn't until it was my turn to be the victim of their vulture-like behavior that I realized what they'd done to the Clarkes.

They benefited from Mr. Clarke's death, just like they would have benefited from my wedding to Vincent. They didn't need me to marry Aiden anymore when they got the trucking business. That, and Mr. Clarke's death made our teenage relationship fall apart.

No wonder everyone paints me with the same brush as my parents. I can't believe I've been so blind.

My mother pulls away and looks me in the eye. She frowns, with that fake smile still painted on her lips.

"Are you okay, pumpkin?"

I blink a couple times and force a smile. "Fine. Just tired, Mom."

"Let's get you inside. I had your old room prepared for you."

All the monologues that I'd prepared disappear from my mind. Now that I'm here, I don't know what to say to her. My father appears in the doorway and grabs my suitcase from my hand. He puts his arm around my shoulder and kisses my temple in a stiff movement. I nod and try to smile again as the three of us head toward my childhood bedroom.

After what seems like an eternity, they finally leave me alone. I close the door and look at the stack of suitcases in the corner. I flop backward onto the bed and stare at the ceiling. My chest feels heavy and my eyes are prickling with tears.

Even after all this, I still haven't had the courage to stand up to them. I've walked right back into my old room and I haven't said a word to them about anything.

I feel like a coward.

I feel like a fraud.

When I was leaving California, I was pumped up full of courage. *This* was my chance to finally stand up to them and tell them what I think. *This* was my time to be my own person and to take back my life.

And yet, here I am. I've come straight back to my old room without saying anything to them. I've let them take me in, and I haven't even told them that I'm mad at them.

It makes me feel like an absolute coward. I take a deep breath to try to relieve some of the pressure in my chest. I squeeze my eyes shut.

I'm almost 30 years old, and I'm living with my parents again. I've run back home after a failed engagement, straight back to the people that used me as part of their business deal gone wrong.

When I open my eyes back up, the tears start streaming down

my face. I can't help it. All the pent-up emotion from my breakup, and from the series of realizations about my family and about myself – it's all coming to a head.

I'm alone. I'm truly, completely alone.

I take a deep breath and blow it out of my nose. I sit up and wipe my face, shaking my head and making a gargled noise as I stand up.

When I fell in the river that day, over a decade ago, Mr. Clarke fished me out and stood me up on the bank. He wrapped me in a towel and looked me in the eyes.

"Are you okay, Mara?"

I remember seeing the little rivulets of water streaming down his cheeks. His hair was plastered to his forehead and his lips were turning blue. His hand was on my arms, rubbing up and down to warm me up. I remember seeing the concern in his face and feeling like his words had real meaning.

Are you okay, Mara?

I can still see his face, as if he was right here in front of me. When he said it, it sounded like he wanted to know the answer. When my mother asked me if I was okay earlier, it was like she was trying to avoid an inconvenience.

No, I'm *not* fucking okay. I'm very, *very* far from being okay.

I grab my jacket and slip out through the sliding glass door at the back of my room. I glance back across my room and I can hear my mother's voice calling for one of the housekeepers. I turn the other direction and slide the door closed again.

As soon as the cool mountain air fills my lungs, my shoulders relax and I close my eyes. I take another breath and let the air cleanse my mind until I can open my eyes again. I look out toward the mountains and feel my heart beat a little bit harder.

I might be alone, but I'm in my favorite place in the whole world. I set off toward the little dirt path behind the hotel and start walking.

I'm alone, and I'm not okay, and I feel like a coward and a failure – but I'm still standing. I glance up the path toward the hill in front of me and I take a deep breath. The crisp air breathes new life into me, and I start putting one foot in front of the other. I tuck my chin into my chest and follow the trail until my mind is clear.

I'm still standing. I'm still walking. I'm still here.

5

DOMINIC

"Did you hear who's back in town?" my brother Ethan says as he walks through the workshop door. I put down my chisel and look up at him with an eyebrow raised.

"Who?" I ask, already knowing the answer.

"Mara McCoy. Without her fiancé, apparently."

"Huh," I say. "She missed the wedding."

Ethan snorts and walks over to my workbench. He leans against it and crosses his arms casually. "Don't think she'd have been invited."

"Aiden's moved on, I think," I reply.

"Not sure you can move on from something like that," Ethan replies.

I grunt and turn back to the chair I'm working on. Ethan watches me for a few seconds before clearing his throat. "How are things with you? Has business picked up at all?"

I raise an eyebrow and look at him. "Not since you asked me that a couple of days ago, no. Why?"

He shakes his head. "Nah, nothing. Sorry. I just thought you were worried about it."

"Well, yeah," I say. I don't know what else to tell him. Of

course I'm worried about my livelihood! I've worked my whole life to be an expert woodworker and furniture maker. Over the past year, I've watched all that work wither away.

"Are you..." Ethan hesitates. "Do you regret it? The hotel, I mean."

I take a deep breath and put my chisel down. I glance up at my brother and sigh. Before answering, I walk over to the mini fridge by the door and pull out two cans of beer. I hand him one and open my own as I consider his question.

"I don't know," I finally answer. "I think it's better for it to be gone. I just didn't expect this kind of backlash."

Ethan makes a noise in response as he takes a long drink of beer. He finishes his sip. "I didn't think people outside of Lang Creek even knew we existed," he says. "Seems like the news travelled a lot further than we thought."

I snort and lift my eyebrows in response. I glance at the progress I've made today – I'm almost done with all the chairs. Pretty soon I'll be out of work.

I lean against the bench, and Ethan and I drink in silence. He glances over at the wall and nods his chin toward the framed carving of the bear.

"They showed me that bear the other day. Maddy did a good job framing it. Looks good."

I glance over at it for the hundredth time today and nod my head slowly. "I had no idea Dad kept all that junk. Aiden was saying there were boxes of it in the attic."

"Yeah. He was proud of you, you know. Dad, I mean. All this?" He sweeps his arm across the workshop. "He'd have loved this."

I look around the room at the tools and stacks of wood. I've got half-built projects that I've designed myself in the corner – a rocking chair, an antique-style side table, a headboard.

"Don't know how proud he'd be to know that I burned it all

down along with that hotel," I say. The bitterness is clear in my voice, and Ethan shakes his head.

"We did a good thing, Dominic. The town would have been filled with tourists. They would have trashed the hotel grounds and ruined the forests. Think of how many endangered species there are in this valley alone! We did it for good reason. Everyone in town agreed."

I grunt and Ethan takes a deep breath.

"All that bullshit about bringing trade to the area was just the McCoys trying to get their money out of it. That's why they didn't tell anyone they owned part of the hotel. One McCoy hotel in town is more than enough. Dominic, you know that, right?"

"Yeah, I know," I snap. I take a deep breath and put my head in my hand. "Sorry. Look, Ethan, I know all that. I know it's for the best. I know everyone except the McCoys were happy about it. I *know* that. But look around you," I say, pointing to the chair I was working on. "That's the last fucking chair I have to make. After that, I've got nothing. No income. No projects on the horizon. *Nothing*. And for what? Maybe if that hotel had been built, business would be booming!"

"You don't know that," Ethan starts.

I shake my head. "I know. *I know!* But then again, I don't know anything! My head is fucking melted."

"Look, what's done is done," Ethan says a little more gently. "The whole town was on our side. We did nothing wrong. The hotel company, the McCoys, the construction company – they all walked away with insurance money in their pockets."

"Well, they're the only ones with money in their pockets," I say with a snort. Ethan grins and shakes his head.

"It'll work out."

"I know. And I know that I can go work for Aiden, or I can find work somewhere else around here. I just..." I look around at my workshop and take a deep breath. The smell of sawdust fills my nostrils and I exhale loudly. "I just really wanted this to work."

"It will," Ethan says. He stares at me straight in the eye. The dark cloud over me lifts ever so slightly as my brother puts his hand on my shoulder. "It'll work out."

I nod, and then crumple my beer can and toss it in the garbage. "I'd better get this chair done."

Ethan follows my lead and finishes his beer. "You coming down to Harold's tonight?"

"Yeah," I grunt. I have no interest in going to the pub tonight and talking to the same people about the same things as last week, but I know that's not what my brother wants to hear. Ethan nods and walks out the door. It's not until I hear the workshop door close and his engine rumble to life that I let out a sigh. Usually my workshop is peaceful and undisturbed. It's where I come to clear my head. Today, it just seems to be making me more confused and more conflicted.

I think of Ethan's words as I pick up my chisel again. *It'll work out.*

I wish I had his confidence.

6

MARA

By the time I've made it to the top of the hill behind the hotel, my cheeks are flushed and my heart is pumping. I'm tired, but it feels good to breathe deeply and to get my blood moving. I stand on the crest and look out over the town of Lang Creek. I can see Harold's Pub, just a few streets down from my parents' hotel. People are milling into the pub already. It's Friday, and Harold will have a live band on later.

My eyes drift down Main Street toward the edges of town. There's a small tendril of smoke coming from the cabin just on the edge of town.

It's from Dominic Clarke's workshop.

I stare at the smoke as it curls and sweeps upwards, finally dissipating into the sky.

Dominic Clarke burned down the new luxury hotel that was supposed to be built last year, and in the process, he ruined my chances with Vincent. I watch the smoke, mesmerized by the wispy streak in the sky.

I should be mad at him. Or at least, I should resent him. But as I watch the smoke curling into the sky, and I imagine him working on the gorgeous furniture he makes, all I feel is gratitude.

He didn't ruin my chances with Vincent. Instead, he saved me from a loveless marriage. He exposed my parents for who they really are.

I take a deep breath of fresh mountain air and stare at the smoke for a while longer.

I wonder what Dominic is doing right now? I wonder if the sweat is staining the back of his shirt, and if he's pushing his thick hair off his forehead. I imagine his face, as best as I can remember it, and something shifts inside me.

This feud – whatever it is – between our two families... it's ridiculous. It's silly. For the past ten years, ever since Mr. Clarke died after saving me, it's split the town in two.

For a long time, the Clarkes were the outcasts. My parents own the local hotel and the trucking company that dominates the area for a hundred miles. They have a lot of pull in town.

When the new luxury hotel burned down, everything changed. Now people look at the Clarke brothers with respect. I heard one man calling them the 'Keepers of Lang Creek.'

A breeze sweeps through the trees and sends a chill through me. I shiver, snapping out of my daze and finally look away from Dominic's workshop. I start back down the path that takes me down the hillside, back toward town.

With every step that I take, my heart feels a little bit lighter. I'm not a coward, or a fool. I trusted my parents, and I trusted my fiancé. I can't fault myself for that. This could be my chance to reach out to the Clarke brothers and make things right.

I could end this feud, once and for all. *That* could be my atonement for Mr. Clarke's death. Maybe, if I can find peace with the Clarke brothers, I can finally let go of this dark cloud that's followed me for ten years.

Aiden is married now, so maybe he'll be ready to forgive me

for falling in the river that day. Even if he isn't, I can do my best to distance myself from my parents' reputation.

By the time I make it back to flat ground, and the McCoy Hotel looms up in front of me, my whole demeanor has changed. The corners of my lips are tugging upwards and there's a bounce in my step. I glance over my shoulder and look at the small peak that I just climbed.

I smile for real as I look over the scenery around me. The familiar feeling of awe and reverence fills me, and I whisper a quiet *thank you* to the mountains. It's not until I slide open the back door that the smile fades. Even through the closed bedroom door, my mother's voice screeches down the hallway. I poke my head out into the hallway and she calls me over.

"Mara! There you are! Come talk some sense into your father!"

I walk slowly toward them, finally rounding the corner to see them on opposite sides of the front desk. My father nods at me. He's a big man, with a round belly hanging down in front of him. His big paws are resting on the counter in front of him and his grey whiskers are trembling as he looks at my mother.

"I was just telling your father that we need to make some sort of change around here."

"We don't have the money, Margaret," my father growls.

My mother huffs. "Tim, please. We got four hundred thousand dollars in the insurance settlement. That should be going toward improving this place or expanding it! Our business is stagnating!"

I watch the two of them face off, flicking my eyes from one to the other. They almost look like strangers to me. My father's hair is grayer than it was before, and I see the wrinkles in my mother's face when she frowns at him. It's like someone's wiped the sheen off them, and now I can see their true selves. They're still my parents, but they're not the decent, hardworking entrepreneurs I thought they were.

My mother turns toward me and lifts her hand toward my father. "Will *you* tell him? Will you tell him that we need to do *something*?"

"We can't just go spending the entire insurance money on this place! We should be investing it in the trucking business. *That's* where the money is!"

My mother makes a noise, and my father stops talking. The two of them turn to look at me, and suddenly it's like I'm the one who's supposed to come up with the answers. I clear my throat and glance from one to the other.

"Well," I answer, choosing my words cautiously. "The hotel is a bit... dated. It could do with some freshening up."

My mother makes a satisfied noise and my father huffs. I hold up my hands.

"It doesn't have to be anything extreme. Didn't the state government expand their budget for National Parks this year? Maybe we can get listed as approved accommodation with the Park?"

"We've tried that," my father says, shaking his head. "There are all kinds of requirements that we don't meet. We need to have the hotel represent 'local culture and heritage', whatever that means."

I try to contain the smile that's drifting over my face. "I could put this expensive Interior Design degree to good use. I worked on a heritage hotel in California, remember? I'm sure the New York requirements will be similar."

Both of them look at me, eyebrows raised. My mother opens her mouth and closes it back up. She blows air out of her nose and shrugs her shoulders as she looks at my father. They exchange a look and then turn back toward me.

"What is it?" I ask. "You don't think I'm good enough to work on this place?"

"No! Of course not, darling," my mother croons. "It's just..."

"That's a good idea, Mara," my father says. He doesn't even try to hide the surprise in his voice. I ignore the flash of annoyance inside me. I've always known my parents thought I was vapid and thoughtless. These things don't surprise me anymore.

The two of them exchange a glance, and finally my father nods. "Alright. We'll put a hundred grand into it."

A grin spreads over my face and I dip my chin down. "I can work with that." I brush past them before they can change their minds. "I'm going to Harold's. I'll be back later. We can go over the details tomorrow."

I don't catch my mother's words as the hotel door slams behind me. Laughter bubbles up through me, and I glance back at the old hotel. This is either the best idea I've ever had – or the absolute worst.

7

DOMINIC

I FINISH SANDING the last of the chairs and stand it up next to the table. All I need to do now is stain and finish them, and then I'll be done with my last job for the foreseeable future.

I almost regret telling Ethan that I'd see him at Harold's. As I look at the table and chairs, I take a deep breath and shake my head. Maybe it'll be good to get out of this workshop. I can have a beer with my brother. I can always leave if I don't want to be there.

After a quick shower, I pull on my jeans and a flannel shirt. I comb my hair with my fingers and pull on a thin jacket before jumping into my truck. It bounces down the gravel road until I turn down Main Street toward the other end of town.

The lights are on at Harold's Pub, and there are cars lined up down the block. People come here from miles around on Friday nights – and that's why I usually avoid it.

Tonight, though, the distraction will be welcome. Maybe, if there are enough people and the noise is loud enough, it'll drown out all the thoughts running through my mind.

I pull the truck up past the pub and hop out, kicking the door closed behind me. The air is cold, and my damp hair starts to feel frosty against my head. I blow out the air from my lungs and turn toward the pub. I'm so focused on getting inside that I don't see Mara McCoy until we're almost crashing into each other as we both reach for the door.

"Sorry!" she says, glancing up at me.

"S'okay," I grunt. She's right beside me, and the faint floral smell of her perfume fills my nose. Her eyes are bright blue and her nose is sprinkled with freckles. She smiles at me shyly.

"Hey," she says. It comes out as a breathy whisper, and her eyes drop down.

"Hey," I respond. My throat feels tight, and I'm not sure why. She reaches up to tuck a strand of wheat-gold hair behind her ear before glancing up at me.

"You going to Harold's?" she asks, nodding toward the door. Her cheeks start flushing and she lets out a laugh. "Stupid question. Sorry. I just... I didn't know you came here."

"I don't," I grunt. "Usually."

She nods once, and I reach toward the door. The noise inside the pub sounds too loud already, but I watch Mara walk in and I follow her anyway. The two of us stand at the bar, and I steal a glance toward her. It's been a few years since I saw her, and I forgot how pretty she is. Did she change her hair? Maybe I just always remembered her as the 14 year-old girl that was dating my brother.

She's so... I don't know... Womanly?

She smiles at Harold behind the bar and leans over to order herself a drink. She nods toward me and Harold nods back. Before I know it, a beer appears in front of me and Mara touches her glass to mine.

"I come in peace," she says with a grin. I can't help smiling back at her and nodding my chin as I take a sip.

"Welcome back," I respond. "Next one's on me."

Her face breaks into a smile and white heat runs down my spine to the pit of my stomach.

"I'll hold you to that, Dominic Clarke."

The way she says my name sends another thrill through my stomach. She grins again and slips away toward a group of girls before I can answer. I watch her walk away until she's with the other girls, hugging them and laughing. Two of them – the Wilson sisters – look over at me and say something to her. I turn my back on the group and bury my face in my beer before Mara glances up at me.

I can imagine what they're saying. They're probably talking about how unusual it is to see me here. How business must be especially bad if I'm in for a drink. Maybe they're talking about the fire... Again. A year later, and it seems to still be the best topic of conversation whenever I'm around.

I sigh and slide onto a bar stool. It groans under my weight and I shake my head. I wonder if any furniture is made for someone my size. Everywhere I go, I tower over everyone. I've gotten very well acquainted with the tops of people's heads. I hardly fit through doorways, and I'm constantly afraid of breaking chairs.

Maybe that's why I became a furniture maker, I think as I take another sip. It had nothing to do with my father – I just wanted things I could sit on without fear of collapse.

A smile is forming on my lips – right up until my brother claps me on the back. My beer sloshes in the glass and Ethan laughs.

"You made it! When you said you were coming down, I didn't quite believe you."

I grunt in response and take another drink. Ethan waves Harold down and starts chatting to him. They talk about the weather, about the Park – about things I wouldn't even notice. Sometimes I wonder how Ethan and I are related. Harold walks away and Ethan turns toward me, leaning casually against the bar. His eyes sweep across the small bar and he grins.

"Mara McCoy is here," he says, nodding his head toward the group of girls.

"I know," I say, staring at the beer she bought me. "I saw her when I walked in."

"She looks good," he says.

"Does she?" I ask, taking another sip of beer. I put the glass down and turn toward her. She glances up at me and the corner of her lip lifts up. My heart jumps in my chest and my cock suddenly feels heavy. Her eyes flick back to one of the Wilson sisters and I turn back to my beer.

Ethan finds someone else to talk to and I sit on my own until my beer is empty and Harold puts a fresh one in front of me. I'm staring at the golden liquid, trying to decide if the noise and people are worth the distraction, when I feel a delicate hand on my arm.

I jump, looking up to see Mara staring at me with those piercing blue eyes of hers. Her pink lips curl into a smile, and I can't help licking my lips. Her eyes flick down and my cock twitches between my legs again.

That beer has gone straight to my head.

She slides onto the bar stool beside me and leans her head on her fist. She smiles at me again.

"So," she says. "Dominic Clarke."

There she goes, saying my name like that again. I look at her, waiting for her to continue. Harold puts a beer in front of her but she ignores it, keeping her eyes glued on me instead.

"It's good to see you," she says. Her words surprise me, so I lift my beer to my lips and take a drink, nodding as I put it back down.

"It is?"

"It is," she says. Her voice is soft, and I have to strain my ears to hear her over the din in the pub. I flick my eyes over to her and nod, surprised to see how sincere she looks. She takes a deep breath and sighs before standing up again.

I'm still scrambling for something to say when she grabs her beer. She puts her hand on my arm again and gives it a light squeeze before slipping away. I look up at the taps of beer in front of me, feeling the emptiness where she was a moment ago. My arm is burning where her fingers were, and the smell of her perfume is still lingering around me. I force myself to keep my face forward, even though every part of me is screaming to turn around.

My heart is thumping and my whole body is tense. It's not until Ethan appears beside me and puts his hand on my shoulder that I start to relax again. He squeezes my shoulder and laughs.

"What was all that about?"

"All what?" I ask, glancing at him.

"You and Mara," he says. I can hear the grin in his voice as I turn back to my beer. "You fraternizing with the enemy?"

"She's not the enemy," I snap. Ethan throws his hands up and laughs. I drain the rest of my beer and stand up, brushing my jacket down. I nod to my brother. "See you later."

"Later," he says. There's still a grin in his voice and his eyes are sparkling with mischief. It annoys me, but I don't know why – and I don't know how to respond. All I do is spin around and walk straight out the door. When the cool air fills my lungs and the sounds of the pub are muted behind the door, I can finally breathe easy again. I glance behind me, still feeling the heat of Mara's gaze.

I shake my head and stalk toward my truck. I shouldn't have come out tonight. I don't understand people, and I usually don't like them. I have no idea what that was about. The last thing I want to do is start people talking about the Clarkes and the McCoys all over again.

I just want to be left alone.

8

MARA

When Dominic leaves the bar, I suddenly don't feel like being there anymore. Tanya Wilson is telling me about her new boyfriend, and I try to fight the feeling that I couldn't care less.

I almost feel the door closing as Dominic walks out, and I glance over at the seat where he sat only a couple seconds ago. My heart is still thumping and my mouth has gone dry. There's an undercurrent of electricity coursing through me from head to toe. As I take a deep breath, I can hardly focus on anything but the delicious thrills buzzing through my body.

When we ran into each other outside, I could hardly think straight. His body is so muscular, it took all my self-control to keep my eyes on his face. When I went to the bar to get another drink, my hands were itching to touch him.

His eyes are a deep brown color, and he was looking at me almost suspiciously. I glance around the bar, wondering how long I'll last in here tonight. The band is playing and people are dancing, but suddenly I just feel like leaving.

I force myself to stay for another drink, and finally say my goodbyes.

"Just tired, long day today," I say when Tanya asks me why I'm going. She nods in understanding and gives me a hug. I extract myself from the group and finally make it out the door, turning down the road toward my parents' hotel.

I walk slowly, taking deep breaths as I stroll down the street. The old-style streetlamps light the way, and I walk by all the familiar shops and houses that I grew up with.

This place has hardly changed, but it feels different. Maybe I'm the one that's changed. Maybe I'm the one that's seeing it through different eyes. I feel like the new hotel burning down and my breakup with Vincent has made me a different person.

The McCoy Hotel is standing proud on the corner in front of me, and I look at the old timber building. I tilt my head to the side as I think about what my parents agreed to.

If they follow through with it, I'll be in charge of renovating this place and getting it approved as a National Park sponsored accommodation. I stop on the corner and inspect the building, welcoming the ideas that start flooding my head. I walk up the flagstone path to the front door and smile as I look at the wide porch. When I swing the front door open, I can picture a fresh, updated design for the lobby.

I walk back to my room without seeing anyone and look around at the standard hotel furnishings that I grew up with. These will all have to be updated as well. I'll have to put together samples and proposals for the application. I put my hands on my hips and smile as my eyes dart around the room.

Get rid of that wallpaper. Replace the blinds. Fresh, cream-colored walls and hardwood furnishings.

I grab a pad of paper and start sketching my ideas, staying up until my eyelids are heavy. Finally, I put the pad of paper on the nightstand and collapse into bed, kicking off my clothes and snuggling under the thick duvet. As I fall asleep, I imagine Dominic Clarke's wide, muscular body. The same current of electricity passes through me until I drift off into a dreamless sleep.

. . .

I SLEEP BETTER than I have in weeks. My whole body feels lighter than it did before. I wake up with a smile on my lips as the sun streams through the window. I roll over onto my side and look at the mountain peaks through my window.

I'm up and out of bed in minutes. I get ready and grab a quick breakfast before heading out on foot. It's a short walk to the edge of town, where I turn down a worn gravel road. My feet crunch on the gravel with every step as I make my way toward Dominic Clarke's workshop.

The doubt starts creeping into my mind as I get nearer to him.

Will he be awake? Should I have called?

I clutch the pad of paper with my sketches to my chest until the little cabin and the huge workshop come into view. My heart starts beating a bit faster when I see the door to the workshop open. I can't hear any tools, and the big garage door is closed, but I can see some lights on inside.

All of a sudden, my heart is bouncing against my ribcage and doubt starts creeping into my heart. What am I doing here? He didn't seem to want to talk to me last night... What makes me think he'd want to see me now? Even though I have no hard feelings against his family, what guarantee do I have that he feels the same way?

I've changed, sure. But everyone else? Everyone else seems to have stayed the same.

I take a deep breath and keep my eyes glued on the open door. It's too late to turn back now. I've already promised my parents a design by the end of the week. I know from experience that the best way to get these projects approved by the Parks is to use local craftsmen.

It's the only way this will work – both for the project, and for me. How else will I make it up to the Clarkes and show my parents that I'm not like them?

By the time I'm a couple steps away from the door, my heart is thumping. My mouth is dry, and a bead of sweat rolls down my spine. My cheeks are flushed and I'm clutching the pad of papers with a vice-like grip. I get to the doorway and take a deep breath before stepping through.

Dominic has his back to me. He's wiping down a gorgeous hardwood chair. It's part of a set of six, as far as I can tell. The back of the chair is an intricate lattice, and the chair legs are perfectly tapered to match the large table beside them.

I breathe out as I look at his work. He glances toward me and stands up, wiping his hands on his rag as he turns toward me. He frowns slightly, taking a step in my direction before pausing.

"Mara?"

"Hi, Dominic," I say. It comes out as a croak, and I can't stop my eyes from wandering from his face down to his chest. His thin t-shirt is clinging to his body in the most delicious way, and that flame in the pit of my stomach grows instantly hotter. He takes a few more steps toward me and I lift my eyes up to his. I can see the question in his look, so I hold out the papers in my hand. He glances down and then back up at me.

He takes a few more steps toward me and takes the papers from my hands. Suddenly, I'm embarrassed. They're not so much sketches as they are scribbles. As I glance around the workshop and I see samples of his work, I feel like a complete amateur.

He's precise, and detailed, and all the bits of furniture that I can see are expertly crafted. He's frowning as he looks at my drawings, flicking through them one by one. My heart is still thumping and all I can think of is how silly he must think I am.

I take a deep breath.

"You think you could make those?"

He finally looks up at me and nods his chin down ever so

slightly. "I could," he answers slowly. His voice is deep, and it seems to reverberate through my chest.

I swallow, letting my eyes drift from his eyes down to his lips and back up again.

"Would you?"

Where has my voice gone? All my words come out as whispers or croaks, and I can hardly stand on my own two feet without feeling like I'm about to topple over. Dominic hands the stack of papers back to me and stares into my eyes. My palms start to sweat, and I resist the urge to squirm. I want him to look away – to stop this torture. At the same time, though, I want him to keep looking at me like that forever.

He finally clears his throat. "Why?"

"Why what?"

"Why do you want me to make them?"

"We're remodeling the hotel," I say. "I'll pay you, obviously! How much would you charge?"

I cringe at my awkwardness. This isn't going how I planned. But how *did* I plan it? I had no idea what I was walking into. My eyes drift down to his shoulders, where the fabric of his shirt stretches across them. His chest is so close to mine I could reach out and touch it. I ball up my fist and take a deep breath to try to control myself. Dominic stares at me for a few moments, and then I see a spark in his eye. The corners of his lips lift up and he starts to chuckle. It's quiet at first, until he's laughing with his mouth wide open. I smile, confused.

He shakes his head and glances at me once more before turning away from me.

"Good one," he says. "I needed a laugh."

He's walking back toward the table and chairs and I rush after him, putting my hand on his arm. A current of warmth shoots up through my hand as I touch him. "Dominic, I'm serious! We're trying to get approved as accommodation for the Park. You're the best woodworker in the state, everyone knows that. I need a new bed and two side tables for every room in the hotel. If we partner together, we could both get recognized as heritage facilities. It's a win-win!"

Dominic frowns and shakes his head, pulling his arm away. The movement makes my heart sting and I take a step back.

"Why do you think I'd help your family? Last time you tried to expand your business, we burned it to the ground, remember?"

The words catch in my throat and we stare at each other. I plead with my eyes, opening my mouth and closing it again. I can still feel the heat of his arm on my palm. I look down at my amateurish sketches and then back up at him.

"I'm not my parents, Dominic," I say quietly. I lift my eyes up to him and see his face soften ever so slightly. He glances back down at the papers and slides them out of my hands. The tips of his fingers brush against mine, and I try to ignore the pulsing in the pit of my stomach.

He's so close to me I can hardly think. I don't know why I'm here. Is it to hire him? Or is it just to be near him? I watch his face as he looks through the drawings again.

Finally, he sighs.

"I'll think about it."

With that, he turns back to the chairs and pops open a can of dark wood stain. I watch him for a few seconds before turning around to walk back outside. The sun is shining brightly now, and I shield my eyes with my hand until I can see properly. The walk back to the main road feels longer than it did on the way in, but maybe that's because all I can think about is the beating of my heart and the heat in the pit of my stomach.

9

DOMINIC

THE SKETCHES MARA gave me are still sitting on the workbench. I can see them out of the corner of my eye as I run my brush back and forth along the top of the table. I try to focus on my work. I watch the stain as it soaks into the oak furniture. I wipe the wood and brush it again to get an even coat, watching the rich, brown color absorb into the grain. The acrid, chemical smell of the stain drowns out any remnants of Mara's perfume.

It'll take me a few days to stain and seal the new furniture, but by the end of the week I'll be done. When the first coat of stain is painted on the table, I stand up straight and stretch my back. I've opened the big garage door, and a light breeze makes the papers on the bench flutter. I stare at them for a few moments before sighing. I walk over and grab the stack of papers, spinning them toward me on the table.

She's got a good eye. The drawings are a bit rough, but I can already see her intent. I flick from one page to another, looking at the precise detailing that Mara has drawn out, and the more general sketches of the finished rooms.

I lean against my worktable and look at all the sketches one by one, shaking my head.

I can't.

I know I can't. I can't work for the McCoys! It almost killed Aiden to work for them until he got his own garage.

And yet, I keep staring at these sketches. I need the work, and a job this big would keep me busy for weeks. If they're getting recognition by the Park, that would put me on the map and it could turn my business around.

If I took the job, I'd almost certainly have to spend time with Mara. My heart thumps at the thought, and I stare at her sketches a bit longer. The breeze washes over me and I can almost smell her perfume again. Long hours, poring over drawings together, late nights together in the workshop...

Shaking my head, I pull myself out of my daydream. I can't lie to myself – I want to do it. I want to make these pieces, and I want to work with Mara, but...

But...

I can't.

Mara is the reason my father died. Aiden would never look at me the same if I took this job. I *burned down* the luxury hotel that her family wanted to build. Do her parents know that she wants to hire me? Are they okay with it?!

The questions are flying around my head, and I just keep staring at the sketches. I flick to the headboard she's drawn up, tracing the gentle curve of it with my finger. I've got a pencil behind my ear, and I grab it and make a few adjustments. I stare at the modified sketch for a few seconds and feel myself start to smile.

The next hour goes by in a flash. I'm grabbing an old piece of wood from the back of the workshop and laying it flat. I'm measuring and sketching and sawing and sanding furiously – glancing at the sketch every few minutes. In record time, I stand up a brand new headboard. It's got the curve that Mara sketched, and some clean grooves and detailing that I added.

I stand it up against the wall and take a step back, feeling the pride swell in my chest. It looks good. I haven't felt that inspired to create something in weeks – maybe longer. I run my hands along the top of the headboard and love how smooth the freshly sanded wood feels under my touch.

"I like it!"

I jump at the noise and turn to see my brother Ethan in the doorway. I was so focused I didn't even hear his car pull up.

"Thanks," I respond, turning away from the headboard and back to the table and chairs.

"You got another job? It looks good," Ethan says, walking toward the headboard and running his hand over it just like I did. I resist the urge to tell him to stop touching it, instead turning back toward the work I'm actually getting paid to do.

"Nah, just playing around with some ideas," I respond without looking up. "What's up? Two days in a row to visit me? Must be important."

I glance up to see Ethan grinning. "Not happy to see me?"

I snort, shaking my head and turning back to my work.

"I just wanted to see how you were doing. You left in a hurry yesterday. Harold's was just starting to go off."

"Had enough of the place," I respond.

Ethan grins. "Enough of eyeing Mara McCoy, you mean?"

I throw him a glance and put my head down to work again. I try not to bristle as Ethan peers over my workbench at the sketches that Mara left behind. He turns a page over and frowns.

"What's this? Did you do these?"

"It's nothing," I say, maybe a bit too gruffly. I grab the stack of papers and stuff them in my back pocket. "I'm fine, Ethan. Just need to get these things done."

Ethan stares at me for a few moments and nods his head. "Alright. I brought you some new firewood, help me unload it?"

I nod, following him out the door. We work silently,

unloading his truck and stacking firewood until he claps me on the shoulder and finally leaves. I watch him drive away and let out a sigh. My shoulders slump down and I rub my temples with my fingers.

I definitely, absolutely, cannot take this job. Even Ethan looking at some rough sketches had me panicking. What if I was actually working with Mara McCoy! I'd never hear the end of it.

I make my way back to the workshop and start closing it up for the evening. Once the big rolling door is closed and everything is put away, I reach back and pull out the crumpled sketches from my back pocket.

I can't take this job.

As much as I want to, as much as it would be good for my business, as much as I want to see Mara again, I just *can't*.

I can't deal with the questions from Ethan, and the disapproval from Aiden. I can't deal with the gossip and chatter that would surely follow. I can't deal with the McCoys. I grab the sketches and toss them into the garbage can, turning my back on them and walking out the door.

After a long shower and a cold beer, I have a mediocre dinner of leftovers and fall asleep on the couch. When I wake up to the grey light of dawn, my whole body is stiff. It aches to get up, and I groan as I put my head in my hands.

I can't get her out of my head.

I dreamt of her last night, and I woke up thinking she was beside me.

I don't know how, or why, but Mara McCoy has gotten under my skin.

10

———

MARA

I WAKE up to the familiar sounds of the hotel. The restaurant is open, and I can hear the pots and pans banging and the cooks calling out to each other. I used to hate being woken up to that sound when I was a teenager, but now it seems somewhat comforting.

It's strange being back home. I lie in bed and take a deep breath, once again wondering how I came to be staying with my parents when I'm almost thirty years old. I try to push away the thoughts that are telling me that my life is falling apart, and to ignore the sense that I've moved backward. My heart squeezes when I think of my failed engagement. I still feel like such a fool for thinking that Vincent cared about me.

I shake my head and swing my legs over the side of the bed. I take a deep breath.

I'm not moving backward. I'm definitely moving forward. Somehow, I've ended up back in my hometown in the heart of the mountains – but in a lot of ways it feels good. I'm away from Silicon Valley and all its fakery. I'm away from my fiancé and all *his* fakery.

When I stand up and stretch my arms overhead, my thoughts

drift to Dominic Clarke. I've never noticed how deep his eyes are, or how he smells ever so slightly of pine. His workshop is incredible. All those half-finished pieces in the corner scream out raw talent.

I walk to the window and open the blinds, casting my eye over the peaks that surround Lang Creek. I lean against the window frame and stare out as my thoughts wander back to the workshop.

Would he ever take the job? I know it's a big ask. I know that our two families have been at odds for over a decade. I know that he probably hates *me* in particular, for falling into the creek that day, and causing his father to get pneumonia. I know his brother Aiden hates me. That alone would be enough to refuse the work.

But still – would he ever take the job? It would be the biggest job he's ever got. I have no doubt. It would set him up to be a supplier for a number of heritage properties. He'd be a fool *not* to take it.

I take a deep breath and shake my head. I already know that's not true. Maybe on paper, it would be a great move – but in practice it would be different. He'd have to work closely with me, and with my parents. He'd have to come to the hotel every week – maybe even every day.

He'll never take the job.

In my heart I know it's true. He's the man who burned down the luxury hotel before it was even built. The hotel would have put Lang Creek on the map. It would have brought a huge amount of people and business to the area.

If he cared about money, he wouldn't have done that.

I take a breath and turn away from the window, trying to ignore the budding disappointment in the pit of my stomach. It's not just the work. I'm disappointed that I won't have an excuse to go to his workshop, and to brush my shoulder against his. I'm disappointed I won't get to look into those deep brown eyes and steal glances at his chiseled body.

By the time I've showered, the sun is warming up the air outside. I can tell it's going to be a gorgeous day, and I glance out the window of my room one more time.

If Dominic Clarke won't build my furniture, I need to find someone who will. With a sigh, I resign myself to the idea of working with someone else. I'll have to atone to the Clarke brothers some other way.

I sweep my eyes around my room and try to find the stack of sketches that I drew. My stomach drops when I remember Dominic taking them from my hands at the workshop yesterday. He's got all of them, even the concept sketches for the rooms.

The thought fills me with a simultaneous sense of excitement and dread. I want to see him again. Before I know it, I'm sliding the glass door at the back of my room open. My feet are taking me back down the road toward the workshop on the edge of town as my heart thumps in my chest.

The air is fresh. There's a bounce in my step as I make my way across town. It's still early, and the town is quiet. I don't pass anyone on my way to Dominic's place, and I'm silently grateful for it. Even going to see him feels like a rebellious move.

After only a few minutes, I'm turning down the long gravel drive that takes me into the edge of the forest. Even though Dominic's cabin is in town, it still feels far removed from it. His house is tucked away at the end of a long driveway, surrounded by dense forest on all sides. I take a deep breath and inhale the fresh air one more time before the cabin and the workshop come into view.

I'm relieved to see the lights on in the workshop. He must be working already. I strain my ears to hear any sounds of tools or saws, but I hear nothing – nothing except my footsteps and the beating of my heart in my ears.

The big garage doors on the workshop are closed, but the small door beside them is open. Every step that takes me closer makes my heart beat a little bit faster.

Should I have come here? I know the answer to that. I'm basically harassing him at this point.

I take a deep breath and shake my head. I'm only here to get my sketches back. I already know he'll refuse the job, so I can just be graceful and leave on good terms.

When I'm two steps away from the open doorway, my heart is hammering in my chest. I close the distance and turn into the workshop, pausing in the doorway and letting my eyes sweep across the big room.

Dominic sees me right away and stands up. He's got a paint brush in his hand, and I can tell he's working on the table in front of him. He's wearing a white mask over his mouth and nose. He lifts the mask off his face and moves it onto his forehead as his eyes narrow.

"Hey," I say.

"Hey," he replies. *God, I love his voice.*

I shift my weight from foot to foot and chew my lip. Suddenly I'm nervous, and I don't know what to say. I take a step toward him almost involuntarily. It's like something is pulling me toward him. My eyes are glued on his, and he stays completely still.

My voice catches when I try to speak, so I clear my throat and try again.

"I was just here to..." Before I can ask him about the sketches, my eyes flick to a huge piece of furniture behind him. It's a headboard, and the curve of it reminds me of what I drew.

My eyebrows knit together and I take another step forward, sweeping my eyes over the headboard. Finally, I drag my eyes back to Dominic's gaze and swallow before opening my mouth.

I take another couple steps toward him so that there's only the half-finished table between us. I look at the headboard again, and

I'm finally able to speak. My voice is hoarse, but I force out the words anyway.

"You made it," I breathe. "You made my sketch."

I make myself glance back at his face. His eyes are dark and unreadable. He's staring at me with an intensity that I've never felt before. My whole body is sparking, and the pit of my stomach is on fire. I can feel the honey pooling between my legs as his eyes burn into mine.

I'm afraid to move, afraid to speak, afraid to breathe. All I do is just stand there and look at him until he finally breaks the spell between us and ever so slightly dips his chin.

11

DOMINIC

HER EYES SHIFT from me to the headboard, and my heart starts hammering against my ribcage. I simultaneously regret making it and want to ask her what she thinks of it. I want her to like it, and I want her to leave and never come back.

I've never been this conflicted.

I watch as she takes a tentative step toward me. She moves around the table I'm working on and walks toward the headboard. I watch her run her fingers over the top of it, feeling the smooth curve the same way I did. She runs her thumb along the beveled groove that I added, inspecting every inch of the piece. Finally, she takes a deep breath and turns toward me. When her eyes meet mine, a jolt passes through my chest.

"It's beautiful," she breathes. "It's better than I imagined."

I grunt. "Thanks."

Her eyes shift back to the wood and she shakes her head. "You're incredibly talented, you know."

I can't help but chuckle. "That's probably why I've got people lining up to buy furniture off me. I'm surprised you could get through the door."

She grins and flicks those blue eyes toward me. The same jolt passes through my chest. She turns toward me, keeping her hands on the headboard behind her. She tilts her head to the side and stares at me curiously.

"Why did you make it? I was sure you'd tell me you wouldn't work with me."

"I don't know. I was sure I'd tell you that too. I still don't know if I want to work with you."

She dips her chin down and grins. "The old feud strikes again," she chuckles.

The corners of my mouth hitch upwards. "'Fraternizing with the enemy', I believe it's called."

Her smile broadens and her eyes stay glued on mine. It feels like my whole body is pulling toward her. All I want to do is press myself against her and tangle my fingers into that honey-colored hair of hers. I want to pull her into me and feel her body against mine. I want to bury my face into her neck and inhale her scent before covering every inch of her skin with kisses. I want to run my fingers over that dusting of freckles on her face and hold her body against mine.

I drag my eyes away from her and turn back toward the forgotten table in front of me. I dip the paintbrush back into the rich brown stain and start brushing it back and forth along the top of the table. I can feel Mara's eyes on me, and the heat of her stare is making my skin prickle.

"Dominic," she says softly.

I grunt without looking up. I keep my eyes focused on the paint brush. It moves back and forth... Back and forth... Back and forth. I don't see her move toward me, I *feel* it. I can almost sense her arm reaching up toward me. I'm like a coiled spring. When she finally touches my arm, an electric current passes through my entire body.

She places her fingers on my arm. She's barely touching me and yet it feels like my whole body is on fire. I stop moving the paint brush and turn my body toward her. She drops her arm and lifts her eyes toward mine. I can see the questions in her stare, but neither of us says anything.

Her eyes are a deep blue, and her lips are full and pink. My mouth is watering as I stare at her delicate features. All I want to do is dip my chin down and press my lips against hers. I want to know how she tastes. I want to wrap my arms around her body and feel her against me. I want to run my hand up her spine and feel the heat of her skin against my palm.

Instead, we only stare at each other. My chest is inches from hers, and I can see it moving up and down ever so slightly with every breath. Her lips part and I wait for the sweet sound of her voice.

"Work with me," she breathes. It's hardly more than a whisper, but it sounds like a shout. Her eyes are searching my face and I can't tear myself away from her gaze. I can still feel the spot on my arm where her fingers touched me, and it takes all my self-control to stop myself from wrapping my arms around her.

Almost as if I'm watching myself do it, I nod once. "Okay," I hear myself say.

Her lips spread in a soft smile and her eyes spark.

"Good," she whispers back. We stay like that, staring at each other – saying a thousand things without saying a word.

I could kiss her. All I'd have to do is dip my head down and I'd get to taste those lips. I could give in to my aching body, reach my arms around her and pull her into me.

I could, but I don't.

Neither of us moves an inch until she nods her head. "I'll come back tomorrow with some real drawings," she says. I watch her walk toward the open door, and before she can leave, I call out to her.

"Mara!" She turns toward me and raises an eyebrow. "Don't... Don't tell anyone. Not yet."

She nods her head down without saying anything and slips outside. It's not until the last hint of her disappears out the door that I finally exhale. I put my hand to my forehead and take a deep breath.

What have I done?

I've just agreed to work with Mara McCoy. No, I've agreed to work with the McCoy family. I've agreed to help them get recognition as official accommodation for the National Park. I've agreed to put them on the map.

I've agreed to do exactly what I've spent the last ten years vowing I'd never condone. Last year I was burning down their new hotel, and this year I'm helping them expand their business.

My cheeks start to burn. The shame and guilt bubble in my stomach, and I stare around my workshop in despair. I can't do this! I can't work with *them!*

But then I picture the way Mara looked when she was running her fingers along the headboard. I touch the spot on my arm where those same fingers touched me, and I picture the way her lips looked when she stood there in front of me.

I know that my brothers would disapprove. I know that the town will talk and talk and talk about it. I know that I shouldn't take the job. I know that nothing good can come of this.

But even though I know all these things, I still want to do it.

I want to feel her touch again. I want to see her smile and I want to smell that sweet perfume. I want to watch the way her lips part when she stares at the pieces of furniture I make, and I want to see the spark in her eye when she looks at me.

I want to be near her, and right now I'd do anything to make that happen. I'll even work with the family that preyed on my brothers and me and stole my father's business. I'll work with the woman that my brothers despise.

My heart is thumping and my cock is heavy between my legs.

My head is buzzing but all I can think of is the last thing she said to me today:

I'll come back tomorrow, she said.

The corners of my lips curl into a smile and I take a deep breath, pulling myself out of my stupor and looking down at the half-finished table in front of me.

I'm going to see her tomorrow, and right now that's the only thing I care about.

12

MARA

FOR THE SECOND time this week, my whole body is buzzing when I make my way back to my parents' hotel. I walk quickly without looking back – trying to make sense of the hurricane of thoughts going through my mind. I do my best to ignore the thumping of my heart and the wetness between my legs, but my body feels like it's on fire.

He said yes!

I can't believe it. I never thought he'd agree. He doesn't want me to tell anyone, which is understandable, but I can still hardly believe he agreed to do it.

I can't even think about the work or the furniture right now. As I walk back through the lush greenery on my way to Main Street, all I can think of is the way he was looking at me. One more second and I would have reached up and crushed my lips against his. I would have fallen into his arms and never let go.

I take a deep breath and glance at the sky above me. This is complicated enough without adding sex to the equation. I'm going to have to find a way to ignore this attraction.

I force myself to think about the hotel. I have a thousand and one things to do for tomorrow if I'm going to be ready to give him drawings. Judging on the quality of the headboard he made in less than a day, neither I nor my parents will be disappointed.

My parents.

How am I supposed to tell them about this? They've given me *carte blanche* to do whatever I want with the hotel, but how will they react when they find out it's Dominic Clarke who's making the new furniture? He's one of the people who burned down the new hotel!

The McCoy Hotel comes into view at the end of the road and I take a deep breath. I'll figure it out. Right now, I have a full list to do, starting with finalizing the designs and starting to procure materials and labor. I want to have the application in to the National Park by the end of the month, which means mockups and drawings of the renovations need to be done as soon as possible.

I spend the rest of the day working, only resting to have a quick bite to eat. I draw up a contract for Dominic and start making proper sketches for him. I work on the rest of the designs – updating the lobby, the dining room, and the hotel bedrooms.

By the time I look up from my desk, the sun has gone down and the stars are out. I lean back in my chair and stretch my neck from side to side, groaning at the stiffness that has set into my body. I stand up and tiptoe to the back of the hotel, slipping into my bedroom and closing the door behind me. That'll have to be enough work for today.

I sit on the edge of the bed, taking a deep breath and kicking off my shoes. I close my eyes and rub my temples when I hear a knock on the sliding glass door. I frown, looking out into the darkness. I see the unmistakable shape of Dominic's huge, muscular body silhouetted in the window and my heart skips a beat.

Getting off the bed, I adjust my clothes and pat my hair back. I take a deep breath and slide open the door. Dominic steps in, and a wave of freshness and pine and sawdust fills my nose. That familiar heat starts growing between my legs and I do my best to ignore it.

His eyes sweep around my room at the messy desk and my childhood bed, and then they finally they rest on my face.

"Dominic," I say, closing the door behind him. "What are you doing here?"

"This is a bad idea," he growls. I search his eyes and see a deep pain inside them. I take a deep breath and try to think of something to say. My fingers drift to his arm and I place them gently on his wrist.

"Dominic..." I breathe. He flinches at my touch and then relaxes, standing completely still in front of me. He seems so out of place in this room. He looks like he should be outside, or in his little cabin on the outskirts of town. It feels like even in a tiny town like Lang Creek, there are too many lights and too many people for him. He's not made to be around other people.

He stares into my eyes and shakes his head from side to side. "My brother would kill me," he finally says. I can hear the pain in his voice and my heart squeezes.

I nod my head slowly. "I understand," I say. I lift my eyes up to his and take a step toward him. My heart is hammering against my ribcage and my mouth is suddenly dry. "Dominic," I say again. "I'm so sorry. About your dad. About my parents. About everything... I...." My voice trails off and my eyes start to prickle. I wish I could make him understand that I'm not the person I was before. I wish I could make him understand that I'm not the person my parents want me to be.

A deep growl rumbles through his chest and Dominic stares deeply into my eyes. "Stop apologizing," he says. His voice is gravelly and deep, and it sends a thrill through my whole body. "It was an accident. I forgave you for that a long time ago."

"You did?" My voice is nothing more than a squeak. Dominic

takes a step toward me, and my hand slides further up his arm. The tips of his fingers touch my waist and my whole body feels like it's about to burst. The desire is overwhelming me. My center is pulsing and the wetness is seeping into my panties as I stare into Dominic's dark eyes. The heat of his body is intoxicating.

I lift my other hand and place it on his chest. His heartbeat pulses against my palm. I can't tell where my heartbeat ends and his begins. We stand there, our fingers barely brushing against each other's bodies, staring into each other's eyes. There's ten years of pain... Ten years of anger... Ten years of things unsaid between us.

"I shouldn't be here," he says. His voice is so low that I feel it more than I hear it. I slide my hand up his arm and brush my fingers along his neck. His chest rumbles and he wraps his arms around my waist, sliding his hand under my shirt so that I can feel the heat of his palm on the small of my back.

I'm melting into him, and I can't do anything about it.

"I shouldn't be here," he says again.

"I'm glad you are," I whisper back. In an instant, his lips crush against mine and his hands are pulling me into him. He slides his hand further up my back so that I can feel the warmth of his skin against me. My whole body is pulsing with desire as he presses his body against mine and kisses me like I've never been kissed before.

This is so wrong. It's *so wrong* and my head is spinning, but somehow, I can't stop. I don't want to stop. I slide my hands over his shoulders and tangle them into his hair, pulling Dominic in for a deeper kiss.

Our families have been at war for a decade. His brothers hate me. My parents used me. I don't know why I'm here, or where I'm going. All I know is that right now, Dominic Clarke's kiss tastes better than anything I've ever tasted before. His body feels like it's made for me, and his hands feel like they know my body better than I know it myself.

My head is spinning, and my heart is hammering, and right now I don't care about anything except Dominic's kiss and the pulsing heat between my legs.

13

———

DOMINIC

I'M NOT sure why I came here. It wasn't for this. It was *never* for this. I wanted to tell her I'd changed my mind... That I wouldn't do it.

But now I'm here and her body is pressed against mine – and all I can think about is how badly I want her. My cock is harder than it's ever been, and when she grinds her hips against me all I want to do is plunge it deep inside her.

I know I shouldn't be doing this. Even if we don't work together, I shouldn't be doing this. Even if she leaves town tomorrow and never comes back, I still shouldn't be doing this.

There's too much history and too much baggage between our families.

But when she runs her fingers along the nape of my neck and presses her chest against mine, all those thoughts disappear from my head. Maybe I shouldn't be here – but it feels way too good to stop.

I drop my hands down toward her ass and pull her into me. She grinds her hips toward me again, and the heat of my erection is burning against me. She moans into me and my cock throbs.

Finally, our lips separate and she's panting. I keep one hand on her ass and bring my other hand between us. I slide it up between her thighs until I can feel the heat of her desire through her pants. I groan, keeping my palm against her center as she whimpers.

Her arms are wrapped around my neck and she pulls her face away from mine. Mara stares at me as I move my palm slowly back and forth between her legs. She lets out a soft moan and my cock throbs at the sound. She closes her eyes and parts her lips, and I dip my head down once again to taste her kiss.

She's trembling. Her body feels like it's going to fall over at any moment, so I wrap my arms around her. I lift her up, and she wraps her legs around my waist. I shuffle over to the bed and lay Mara down, letting the weight of my body press down on top of her. She runs her fingers through my hair, wrapping it into her fist and pulling gently as I groan.

"You're the sexiest woman I've ever seen," I growl. I press myself into her as she grinds her hips against me, letting out a soft moan.

Mara parts her lips and kisses my neck, biting it gently as I peel her clothes away from her collarbone. I want to know every part of her. I want to kiss every inch of skin that I come across. I want to remember every detail of her body.

She reaches down and grabs the hem of her shirt, lifting it up over head. Then follows a flurry of undressing. I'm pulling off my clothes, she's pulling off hers until we're both down to our underwear. She wraps her arms around me again and I crush my lips against hers, grinding my cock against her center.

The feeling of her skin against mine is exhilarating. It makes me feel like I'm drunk. She runs her fingers down my back and across my shoulders as I trail kisses down her neck and between her breasts. I run my hands over her stomach and feel my way over her entire body. My fingers leave trails of sparks everywhere they touch, and my heart is beating so fast I feel like I'm going to collapse.

She runs her hand down my stomach toward my hard cock, but I pull away. I glance up at her face to see her eyebrows shooting upwards. I grin and shake my head.

"Not yet," I growl. "You first."

My kisses take me all the way down the soft skin of her stomach to the fabric of her panties. I love the way she shifts her hips toward me and exhales when my mouth gets nearer to her center. I let the heat of my breath wash over her skin as I move toward her inner thigh, laying soft kisses on her skin as she parts her legs for me. I run my fingers over her panties, feeling the heat of her desire through the thin fabric.

She shifts her hips toward me again and I look up at her – grinning as she bites her lip.

"Dominic," she breathes.

I slide my finger under her panties and feel her sweet honey gathering in her folds. My cock throbs between my legs, but I let my fingers move ever so gently back and forth. She makes that irresistible whimpering sound once again, and I kiss the inside of her thigh.

I've never wanted anyone this badly. My whole body is on fire, and all I want to do is rip the last shreds of clothes off her and take her right now. I'd plunge my cock into her and fill her with my seed in an instant.

And yet, when I look up at her face and see the pleasure washing over it, all I can do is keep moving my hand back and forth. I push the fabric out of the way and dip my head down toward her slit. I kiss her gently, letting my tongue slide out to taste her desire.

She moans as I taste her again, a little bit deeper this time. I find her bud and kiss the little bundle of nerves until her whole body quivers. Her fingers are wrapped in my hair as I gently slide my tongue around her sensitive bud.

She's whimpering and trembling as I explore her body for the first time. I hook my fingers into her panties and slide them down her legs, dragging my eyes back up toward her glistening center. My head dives back down and she fists her hand into my hair, arching her back and grinding her hips up toward my face.

This is more erotic than I could ever describe. She tastes better than anything I've tasted before, and I can almost feel her pleasure in my own body. I kiss and lick and taste and devour, until she's trembling underneath me, grinding her hips up toward my face and pressing my head down toward her.

When I slip my fingers inside her, Mara's whole body contracts. I give myself to her completely, moaning with her as her walls squeeze my fingers and her back arches. She gasps and moans, shoving her hand in my hair and pressing her hips up toward me.

My lips are covered in her wetness, and I don't stop eating her until she relaxes. I lay one more soft kiss at the top of her slit and finally look up at her beautiful face.

Mara's eyes are closed, and her hand is thrown across her face. Her chest is heaving up and down, and I kiss her hip once more before lifting myself up toward her. She opens her eyes and looks at me, shaking her head from side to side.

"Dominic," she breathes. "That was…". She shakes her head again. The corners of my lips curl upwards and I start to chuckle.

"That was fucking *hot*," I finish for her. She grins and nods her head. Her fingers find the sides of my face, and she pulls me toward her to share another kiss.

14

MARA

MY BODY FEELS like it's on fire. Vincent never touched me the way Dominic just did. No one ever has, really. The way he runs his hands over me feels like he's known me for years. Even now, as I tremble and recover from the intensity of my orgasm, he trails his fingers over and back across my chest. His touch sends shivers through my torso.

My heart is pounding, and I take a deep breath to try to slow it down. I turn my head and see him staring at me. I can't help but grin as a blush spreads across my cheeks.

"Dominic," I breathe.

He leans down and presses his lips against mine, hooking his hand around my waist. I wrap my arms around his neck and moan into his lips as we kiss – our arms and legs intertwined on my bed. His lips are soft and he kisses me slowly, groaning as he tastes my mouth.

Dominic shifts his weight and presses himself down on top of me so his erection is pressing against my stomach. I tilt my hips to feel it and he groans in satisfaction. He runs his fingers down my side and cups my ass, guiding my legs until they're wrapped around him.

We're closer than I could have imagined. It feels like every part of me is touching him – like he's wrapped around me and I'm wrapped around him, both so tight that I never want to let go. I kiss his neck. He groans in response, sending a thrill straight through my core. The heat of my desire is blossoming once again as he slides his shaft through my wetness.

The feeling of his cock against me is driving me wild. I press my hips up toward him to feel it against me, and it sends an aching need through my core. I want to feel it inside me. I want to feel *him* inside me. I want him to take me right now.

It doesn't matter who he is, or who I am, or who our families are. All that matters is his body, and my body, and *our* pleasure. All that matters is the way his hand is tangling into my hair, and the way my fingers are sinking into his shoulders. All that matters are the groans he's making every time I touch him.

I'm more alive than I've ever been before. I'm flying. I reach over to my bedside table and grab a condom. Dominic looks from the condom to me and his eyes spark. His chest rumbles as he takes the crinkling package from me.

"You sure?"

"Never wanted anything more," I breathe. I watch as he kneels in front of me on the bed and rolls the condom onto his hard cock. It glides on smoothly, and once it's on, he grabs his cock and drags his eyes up to mine. My whole body is on fire. I bite my lip and look at Dominic, letting my eyes wander from his dark eyes down to his muscular shoulders. His chest and abs are almost gleaming in the moonlight from the window. I reach up and run my finger down the center of his torso until I hit the base of his shaft. I wrap my hand around his thickness and savor the fire that floods my veins.

Dominic groans and tilts his head back as I grip his member, pushing his hips down toward me as I open myself up to him. My legs fall apart and I tilt my hips up to accept him. When the tip of his cock presses against my opening, my whole body relaxes and a moan escapes my lips.

I can't describe the feeling of Dominic's cock. It's better than I can put into words. My body stretches to accept him and grips his girth as he pushes into me. It's like he fits inside me so perfectly that nothing else can compare.

A gasp escapes my lips as he pushes himself deeper and deeper inside me. Inch by inch, he enters me. My walls contract around his girth and I moan once more.

When he starts to pump his shaft in and out of me, I'm already there. The orgasm is building in the pit of my stomach, and I know that in a few instants I'll be flying off the edge. With every thrust of his cock, the pressure in my core builds and builds until my body is no longer under my control.

With one more thrust, Dominic grunts and it reverberates through my chest. The pressure finally releases and the pleasure floods my veins. My back arches as the pleasure courses through my body – over, and over, and over, in wave after wave of bliss.

I don't know if I'm screaming or if I'm silent. I don't know if I'm grabbing on to Dominic's shoulders, his neck, or the bedsheets. I don't know what's happening. All I know is that the intensity of my orgasm is unlike anything I've ever experienced. My whole body contracts around him until he grows harder and starts to tremble with me.

The sweetness of our release is indescribable. He's panting into my ear as I grip onto him. I run my fingers along Dominic's skin, through the thin sheen of sweat that our lovemaking has produced.

When he collapses on top of me, I'm as spent as he is. For a few blissful moments, the only sounds in the room are our heart-beats and our long, ragged breaths.

Finally, I'm able to think again. It's like a fog lifts from my eyes and I see Dominic again for the first time. This time, he doesn't seem like the rugged mountain man that lives on the edge of town. He doesn't seem like a renegade – like the man who has opposed my family for a decade.

He seems calm, and loving, and gentle. He seems so *real*. I run my finger down his cheek and I scratch the stubble on his jaw, and he groans in satisfaction. His eyelids flutter open and he studies my face for a few moments.

"You're beautiful, Mara McCoy."

"So are you, Dominic Clarke," I answer with a grin.

A smile spreads across his face and he closes his eyes again. He tilts his chin toward me as I run my fingers over and back along his jaw. I watch him for a minute, or an hour, or an eternity – until sleep takes us both.

15

DOMINIC

I WAKE up to the gray light of dawn streaming through the open blinds. I don't recognize anything around me. My heartbeat immediately starts to race as I look around the room through my bleary eyes. Finally, I see Mara sleeping beside me and the memories of last night flood my mind.

"Shit," I say under my breath. I crane my ears to try to hear any noise in the hotel. Everything is dead quiet. Mara stirs beside me and her eyes flutter open.

"Hey," she mutters, seeing me awake. "You okay?"

"I'm fine," I answer, running a finger along her cheek. "I should go."

"So soon?" She asks, opening her eyes a bit wider. She lifts her head to look at me and then at the window. "Stay."

I smile. "I wish I could. You know what kind of drama that would cause."

Mara snorts and closes her eyes again. "Five minutes," she says as she throws her arm over me.

"Fine," I whisper, happy to let myself be convinced. She rests her head on my shoulder and nuzzles into me. I run my fingers through her soft hair and kiss the top of her forehead. She murmurs in response. I lie back and stare at the ceiling of Mara's bedroom.

How did I get here?

This wasn't what I was expecting when I came here last night. I was going to tell her that the deal was off. I was going to tell her that no matter what she offered me, I couldn't do business with her. I was going to ask her to not come back to the workshop.

And now?

Now I'm in her bed. I had the most amazing sex of my life. Calling it just 'sex' feels wrong – it was so much more than that. It was like we'd known each other our whole lives. I mean, we *have* known each other our whole lives. But it was like we've *known* each other our whole lives. Like I'd spent the last three decades getting to know her body as well as I did my own.

She sighs, draping her arm across my chest and moving her fingers ever so slightly back and forth along my collarbone. I catch her fingers in my hand and press my lips to them.

I don't know how this happened, and I don't know what it means, or where it will go. What I do know is that right now, with Mara in my arms, I feel *good*. I feel good for the first time in years. I feel like I belong here – or like she belongs with me.

A noise makes me turn my head toward the door. It sounds like someone in the restaurant kitchen. I take a deep breath and lift Mara's arm off me. She opens her eyes again and groans.

"Fine," she sighs.

"I'd stay if I could," I say, kissing her lips. I slip out of bed and pull my clothes on as the chill in the air hits my skin. Mara lifts her head onto her palm and watches me as I get dressed. She smiles and shakes her head.

"I'm not sure what just happened, but I can't say I'm upset about it."

A smile breaks across my face and a chuckle starts to bubble up inside me. "I feel the same way."

I hop on one foot to get my shoe on, and my backside hits her desk. Pens and pencils start rolling off onto the ground. "Shit," I say under my breath, trying to catch them. I catch two before they fall, but most of them fall onto the ground. Mara laughs.

"Sorry," she says. "I should really get a pencil holder."

"Why do you need so many?" I ask with a grin as I lean over to pick them up. "There's got to be two dozen pens and pencils here."

"I like to have options," she says. I glance over at her and see her laughing. I chuckle as I hold up two fistfuls of pencils, shaking my head and putting them back on the desk.

She shrugs. "Just a little quirk you're going to have to put up with," she says.

I lean down and place another kiss on her lips. "I can deal with a few pencils if it means I get to spend another night like that," I say. Her eyes shine and her cheeks blush. I kiss her again. "I'll text you later."

"Okay," she answers with a soft smile. With one more look at the beautiful woman before me, I turn to the back door and slip outside.

The air is brisk, and I bury my chin in my chest as I make my way toward the nearby trees. I'll circle back toward my cabin through the woods, where there's less chance I'll be seen. The last thing I want to do is start rumors – especially if I'll be taking this contract with the McCoys. I may be conflicted about all this, but I do know one thing: I know exactly what my brothers and the townspeople will think if they find out Mara and I slept together.

By the time I'm in the trees, my shoulders start to relax and I take a deep breath. A hint of a smile plays on my lips and I inhale the fresh morning air.

I wasn't expecting this. There's a tendril of guilt inside me – the McCoys are basically our sworn enemies, after all. Aiden dated Mara when they were teenagers. She was the reason Dad got pneumonia and died. Her parents tricked us into signing over the family trucking business. I burned down their new hotel.

There are so many things telling me to leave Mara alone – to run as far away as possible and to keep my quiet life on the edge of town. There are so many things telling me this is a bad idea. How will my brothers react? How will the town react? How will Mara's parents react?

But then I think about Mara's smile when she woke up, and the way her golden hair looked against the white pillows. I think of her face when I made her come for the first time, and the way her fingers dug into my back last night. I think of how good it felt to wake up next to her, and the guilt starts to go away.

Our families have been at odds for a long time, but that doesn't mean it needs to stay that way. Maybe this contract is an opportunity to mend things – and even though Aiden dated Mara when they were teenagers, it doesn't mean she's off limits. He's married now! He wouldn't mind me being with her now, over a decade later.

As soon as the thought crosses my mind, I know it's not true. Aiden took our father's death the hardest. He always blamed Mara for the accident, and still hasn't forgiven her. I don't think so, anyway. Any time her name is mentioned, a cloud passes over his face.

Does that mean I shouldn't get involved with her?

I take another deep breath and wind my way along the path through the trees until I start to recognize the forest around my cabin. Even though summer is coming, the early morning is still quite chilly. The tips of the tree branches are covered in frost, and I take another deep breath as the thoughts swirl around in my head.

I don't know what I should do. I don't know how Aiden or Ethan would react to all this.

All I know is that by the end of today, I'll be out of work. Mara is offering me the biggest contract of my life to redo the McCoy hotel furniture. I have to separate that from last night. Even if I can't get involved with her, I still need to consider this job.

Something stirs in my chest, and I know that I won't be able to separate the two so easily. I know that next time I see her, I won't be able to resist putting my hand around her waist. I know that her lips will call out to be kissed, and my body will be drawn to hers like a magnet.

I know all these things, but I tell myself I just need the work. That I'm just taking this job because I need the money. The fact that Mara and I slept together last night is irrelevant.

... right?

16

MARA

I CAN'T KEEP the smile off my face today. I get up and hum to myself as I get ready. I sing in the shower and I smile as I get dressed. When I'm ready, I grab my drawings and make my way out to the dining room where I know I'll find my parents. Sure enough, they're sitting at their usual table having their morning coffee.

"Good morning!" I call out.

My mother looks up from the newspaper and furrows her brows.

"What's gotten into you?"

"What do you mean?"

"You're in a good mood," she says, leaning back in her chair and raising an eyebrow.

I laugh. "Is that not allowed?"

My father scoffs and motions to the chair beside him. "Have a seat, Mara. Coffee?" He motions to the pot of coffee in the middle of the table. I nod in thanks and pour myself a mug. He lets me sit down before speaking again. "We were just talking about the renovations. We'd like to see some drawings soon. Will you be applying to the Parks this week?"

I slide into the chair and put the folder of sketches on the table. "That's what I've come up with so far. The concept is to maintain the hotel's natural heritage while highlighting some of the nearby mountains. The color scheme is based on the land-scape," I explain as my father thumbs through the drawings.

He passes some papers over to my mother who inspects them with a critical eye. She makes a noise and purses her lips.

"Are you sure about this, Tim? So much work – and right before our busiest time of the year!"

My father looks through the drawings one more time and glances at me. "You think you can get us recognized by the Parks?"

I gulp. Not only would this be the biggest job I've ever designed, but it's for my parents. This won't be any regular client-designer relationship. My heart thumps when I think of last night and all the trouble I could get myself into.

I nod my head. "We can. With these updates, we'll be in the boutique hotel category, and we'll have enough heritage elements to get certified. There's no reason not to go for it."

My father nods and shifts his eyes back to the papers.

"All this furniture – is this custom made?"

The question seems innocent, but I've been preparing for it for the last two days. I swallow and nod, trying to keep my voice steady.

"Custom made and designed. We have to have a certain percentage of work done by local people." I pause. "What about Dominic Clarke? He's talented –"

"Absolutely not," my mother says, dropping the papers and leaning back. She shakes her head from left to right and lifts her hands up. "No. You want to hire that brute to work on *our* hotel? The one who ruined our chances of expanding the business? No."

My father looks at my mother over his glasses and then

glances back at the drawings. When he says nothing, I take a deep breath.

"Having the furniture maker in town would be –"

"*No*."

The finality in my mother's voice makes me stop. I nod once and take a sip of coffee. My heart is hammering in my chest and I try to keep my cheeks from burning. I knew it would be a battle to get them to hire Dominic, but it sounds like it's not even an option. I take another sip of coffee and watch the dark liquid swirl in the cup.

I can feel my parent's eyes on me, and I try to keep my face steady. Dominic was right. This whole thing is a bad idea. I should have listened to him – he lives here! I've been away from Lang Creek for ages. I've forgotten how things work around here. I should have listened when he told me it would never work.

Now I have to either hide it from my parents or convince them to hire their sworn enemy. I glance up at the two of them to see them staring at me. I force a casual smile and nod my head.

"I'll do some research and find another local furniture maker," I say.

My mother nods and purses her lips as she picks up her coffee mug. "We won't have that savage anywhere near our business." She pauses, glancing at my father with a raised eyebrow. "Will we, Tim?"

My father makes a noise in agreement, but keeps his eyes trained on me. He frowns slightly and stares at me for a few moments before turning back to the newspaper in front of him.

My heart is hammering in my chest. He knows something's up. He can tell something is going on, but he just won't say it. I throw back my coffee and get up, nodding to my parents and grabbing the papers before shuffling out of the dining room.

By the time I'm in the office, my head is spinning. I want to hire Dominic. Not only is he in town, he's the most talented woodworker I've ever seen. And last night...

I need to see him again. I need to spend time with him. I've never felt as good as I did waking up next to him this morning.

My parents will come around. They'll understand eventually. They'll see that this feud between our two families is ridiculous, and it's all our fault. If I hadn't fallen in the river and if they hadn't bought out the Clarke Transportation business, then none of this would have happened.

Dominic, Aiden, Ethan – they've done nothing wrong. They reacted exactly how a normal person would react if their father died and they were betrayed by the only other adults in their life. I can't fault them for that. They were used exactly how I was used with Vincent.

I don't know why I'm working for my parents now, or why I still want their approval. I don't know why I'm here, or what I'll do once these renovations are over.

I'm lost. The only thing that feels right is being with Dominic. The only thing that feels like it makes sense is spending time with him.

What if we could fix this? What if we could end this feud, and bring our two families back together? What if I could make a better name for my family, and show that I have integrity and that I have a heart?

I make it to my room and flop back down on the bed. I can still smell Dominic in my sheets, and I take a deep breath. I exhale as I close my eyes, imagining his hands all over my body.

I'm not ready to let that go. I'm not ready to give up yet another part of my life just because my parents said so. It's time for me to live life for myself.

17

DOMINIC

WHEN I DELIVER the finished table and chairs, it feels like there's a sense of finality to it. They turned out well, and I'm proud of the work I've done. I drive back to the workshop and clean everything up. I put all my tools away and sweep the sawdust off the floor. I wipe the workbench down and stack the scraps of wood in the back of the shop.

Once everything is clean, I stand near the door and sweep my eyes around the room. It's spotless, which is not the way I like my workshop to look. Usually I have a half a dozen projects going on, in various stages of completion.

The headboard I made the other day is leaning against the far wall, calling out to me like a beacon. Nothing else has come up, and right now it seems like my best and only option. I run my fingers through my hair and make the long walk to the other side of the workshop toward the headboard.

I run my fingers along the top of it, exactly how Ethan did. Exactly how Mara did. I look at the piece that I threw together and the corners of my lips start to lift up.

I want to take this job.

As much as I've been telling myself I shouldn't, or I don't want to, or that no one would approve, I know that I want to take the job. I want to spend the next few weeks working furiously and then have something at the end of it that I'm proud of. I want to collaborate with Mara and spend more time with her. I want to see her every day, to hear her laugh, and see that spark in her eye.

I want to do this.

I almost jump when I hear her voice behind me. I turn to see her in the doorway, grinning at me.

"Admiring your work?" she asks.

I chuckle. "Something like that."

"I don't blame you." She's wearing a flowing dress that falls just above her knees. It fits her perfectly, and I can't help but stare as she walks toward me and puts her hands on my chest. I dip my chin down and press my lips against hers. Her hands slide up around my neck and we embrace as our bodies melt together. She pulls away and smiles at me.

"So, I have some bad news," she starts.

My eyebrows jump up. "You don't seem too upset."

"Well, I'm not. The bad news is my parents don't want to hire you."

"Okay," I respond. I wait for her to continue.

"The good news is, I don't care."

I laugh and wrap my arms around her waist. She interlaces her fingers behind my neck and lifts her eyes up to mine. I can see a spark of mischief in her eyes that I recognize from when we were kids.

"That's very brave of you," I say.

She tilts her head to the side and grins. "I'm a brave person."

"I know you are," I growl. "You're here with me, all alone." She grins as I dip my head down toward her and kiss her again, this time a little bit harder. I never knew it could taste so good to kiss a woman. I never knew that having someone in my arms could feel so right. I never knew what I was missing until she walked into my workshop and offered me the world.

She presses herself against me and pulls my neck down toward her. I run my hands down her sides and around her body. I love the way she fits into me. She makes a little moan and my whole body trembles. I drag my hands down to her ass and grip it, pulling her closer to me. My cock is hard again, and I know she can feel it pressed up against her.

I lift her up and sit her down on the workbench. She yelps and giggles, keeping her arms wrapped around my neck.

"I want you," I say. My voice is gravelly, and when I speak, I see a spark in her eye. She grins.

"So take me."

She reaches for her purse and I see her take out the unmistakable silver package of a condom. My heart starts pounding and I take it from her. In an instant, my pants are around my ankles and the condom is on. She wraps her legs around me and I reach up her skirt. My eyebrows shoot up and she laughs.

"No panties?" I breathe.

All she does is bite her lip in response. I can't take it anymore. I'm like an animal. My cock plunges deep inside her in one smooth motion and we both moan at the same time. Her walls stretch for me and I exhale as I enter her. I push myself deep inside her until we're completely connected. Her fingers dig into my shoulders and she throws her head back in ecstasy. I stare at the curve of her neck as I drive my cock deeper and deeper inside her.

Anyone could walk in. Anyone could hear us through the wide-open door. She's sitting on the workbench in plain view, with her legs wrapped around me and her dress pushed up around her waist. Anyone could catch me, Dominic Clarke, with Mara McCoy in the throes of passion – but I don't fucking care.

No part of me cares right now. All that matters right now is Mara's pleasure and the heat building in the pit of my stomach.

When she comes, it's too much for me. My orgasm explodes and I savor the feeling of her fingernails digging into my back. Pleasure floods my veins and I groan, letting myself go completely. She grabs onto me, resting her head on my shoulder as her legs are locked around my waist.

It takes a couple minutes for the breath to come back to my body. She lowers her legs and we separate as I discard the condom. When I pull my pants back up, she's adjusting her dress. She flicks her eyes toward me and grins.

"Good morning," she says with a laugh. "That was nice."

"It was better than nice," I respond. I tangle my fingers into her hair and bring my face to hers. I kiss her once more as she wraps her arms around my neck and presses her body against me.

I can't get enough of this woman. She's incredible and sexy and smart and funny... all I want to do is spend my days with her.

A little voice at the back of my mind is screaming that it's a bad idea, but I can't help myself. When she pulls away from me, she runs her finger along my jaw and scratches my beard. I close my eyes and groan. Her touch feels so, so good. Her body feels like it was made for me. Her kiss tastes incredible. I ignore that little voice and wrap my arms around Mara, bringing my lips to hers once more.

18

MARA

"YOU WANT TO HAVE SOME LUNCH?" he asks, nodding to the door. My eyebrows shoot up and a smile floats onto my lips.

"Are you asking me on a date?"

Dominic grins. "Is that allowed?"

"Treading on dangerous territory there," I respond with a laugh. "What would my parents say?"

"Whatever they want," he responds as he wraps his arm around my waist. "I'll make you some food."

"Can you cook?"

"I can try," he responds with a laugh. He leans down to kiss me before pulling away. He gestures out of the workshop toward the cabin, and I follow his lead. Dominic puts his arm around me, resting his hand on the small of my back and a thrill passes through my spine. I can't stop smiling.

When we get to the cabin, he starts a fire in the wood-burning stove as I look around. The cabin is small, but it's impeccably clean. I wander over to a shelf and see a row of photos. I frown, pointing to one of them, laughing.

"I remember that day!"

Dominic glances up from the fire, closing the door to the

stove. He walks over to me and I smell the faint smell of smoke on his clothes. He leans over to look at the picture and grins.

"The fair was in town. You started crying when a clown came up to you," he says, glancing at me and chuckling.

My cheeks start to burn as I remember that day. I couldn't have been older than seven or eight. I'd been so excited to go to the fair, but when I got there I was overwhelmed by the lights, and colors, and people, and I'd started crying.

"You won me a teddy bear," I say softly. The memories of that day start flooding in and I smile. Dominic puts his arm around me.

"I just wanted you to stop your wailing," he laughs. I laugh in mock outrage and smack his arm. He looks at me with soft eyes and nuzzles his nose against mine. "It's nice to see you again, Mara."

"I missed you. You and your brothers, I mean. After the accident." Dominic keeps staring at the photo but his body stiffens beside me. I shake my head. "Sorry. I shouldn't have said that."

"No," he says. His voice is soft. "It's okay. I missed you too. It was like all of a sudden we lost our Dad and you *and* your family."

"I'm sorry," I say. My eyes start to mist up and I look down at the ground. Dominic turns to me and tilts my chin up. His eyes are bright. For a few moments, he says nothing. The only noise is the popping of the logs in the fire. Finally, he shakes his head.

"Stop apologizing," he breathes. "You did nothing wrong."

"If I hadn't been playing on the edge of the river..."

Dominic shakes his head. "Stop," he whispers. "I told you, you did nothing wrong." My eyes start to tear up and he wraps his arms around me. I melt into him and he rubs my hair and kisses the top of my head. Finally, he pulls away and looks at me again.

"I blamed you for Dad's death for a long time. I thought you betrayed us. But Mara," he pauses, wiping a tear from my cheek.

"I feel so lucky that you've come back. I've just started spending time with you, but I already know that you're an amazing woman. The biggest mistake my brother ever made was letting you go."

The tears are streaming down my face and I make an awful sobbing, snorting sound. Dominic chuckles and wraps his arms around me again. He makes soft noises and holds me until my sobs slow down. Finally, he pulls away and looks at me with a glimmer in his eye.

"It's worse than the carnival day in here," he says.

I snort-laugh again and look at him through teary lashes. "Got any more teddy bears for me?" I ask. Dominic chuckles and slides his fingers into mine. He leads me to the couch and I rest my head on his shoulder. We watch the fire blazing in the stove for a few moments until I speak again.

"My parents used me too, you know. My engagement to Vincent – it was all part of a business deal. When the new hotel burned down last year, it all went to shit. Like an idiot, I didn't even realize what was going on. I can't imagine what it must have felt like for you and your brothers. You were all so young..."

Dominic grunts. "Sorry about the hotel thing. That's probably partly my fault."

I laugh. "Is that an admission of guilt?"

Dominic turns his head toward me and I see the smile playing in his eyes. "Didn't realize you were a lawyer as well as an interior designer."

"I'm a woman of many talents," I respond. His eyes spark and a shiver passes down my spine. I've learned to love his eyes. In the light of day, they look pale – almost hazel. When it gets darker out, or when he's thinking, they get so dark they look like inky pools. Right now, his eyes are bright and they're crinkling at the corners.

"If burning that hotel down brought you back here, then I'm not actually sorry at all," he growls. My heart leaps in my chest and before I can answer he catches my lips between his. He runs his fingers through my hair and pulls me close. I wrap myself around him and press my body against his, loving how strong and solid he feels when he holds me.

We make love. Our bodies fuse together, and for the second time today I'm carried out of my body and into a tidal wave of pleasure. When he touches me, it feels like my skin is sparking and crackling. When he kisses me, it feels like my body is set on fire. When he enters me, I am complete.

For the first time in years, I'm completely at peace. Dominic Clarke doesn't hate me. He doesn't blame me for his father's death. He accepts me for who I am and understands me in a way that no man ever has.

I'm more comfortable and at home with him than I have been anywhere else. His arms were made for me. His body molds and curves perfectly to fit against mine. The day and evening go by like a dream, with laughter and food and sex, and finally ends with a deep, blissful sleep.

In that little cabin on the edge of town, on a weekday evening like any other, I feel like I've finally found peace and contentment.

19

DOMINIC

MARA IS different than I remember, but she's also the same. When we were kids, she used to be fearless but clumsy at the same time. Now, she's still got that fire deep inside her, but it's more tempered. She's not as impulsive as she was when we were little. She's graceful. She moves with purpose, and her intelligent eyes seem to take in more of the world than I knew existed.

She's snoring gently beside me, and I watch her chest rise and fall as she sleeps. I brush a strand of hair away from her face and watch her for a few moments.

I'd never considered that her parents might have used her just like they used us. They were probably using her when they encouraged her to date Aiden. They've never wanted her to be happy – they just wanted my father's business.

When he got sick, they didn't need her to marry Aiden anymore. They could acquire my father's business directly without waiting for the three of us to inherit it. They could get all of it instead of only a third. All they had to do was pretend they were buying it from us to help us with hospital bills.

I blamed Mara for a long time, and then I blamed Dad for not going to the hospital sooner. I blamed Mara's parents for betraying us, and then I blamed myself. I was the eldest, after all. I should have known not to sell them the business.

Mara snorts in her sleep and shifts, making a small noise and going still again. I smile, pressing my lips to her forehead.

In all the years that I blamed the McCoys for our hardships, I've never considered that Mara could have suffered as much as us. At least my brothers and I had each other. Mara was on her own, with parents who didn't care about her and half the town thinking she was to blame for my father's death.

I wrap my arms around Mara and hold her close. My heart seems to grow in my chest as she sleeps against me, and all I want to do is keep her warm and safe. I fall asleep like that, with my arms holding her close. Our breath mixes together as we drift to sleep in my small bed.

SHE STIRS BESIDE me and I wake up, opening my eyes to see her smiling at me.

"Morning," she says. Her voice comes out as a croak, and she laughs before clearing her throat. "Morning," she says again.

"Morning, beautiful."

Her cheeks flush a little and I smile. In this light, I can see the smattering of freckles across her nose. Her eyes are clear and bright.

"I don't know about you, but I'm starving," she says.

"Is that so?" I ask, not ready to get out of bed. I drape my arm across her body and she giggles as I pull her close. My cock is aching for her, and she gives me a little grin as she presses her body against mine.

"Maybe I can wait," she says. I crush my lips against hers and groan as she wraps her arms around me. If I could stay in bed forever with her, I'd be happy. Waking up next to her in my bed is the sweetest pleasure I could ask for. When I watch her head lean back and her lips part – when her back arches and her body contracts around mine – I feel like the luckiest man alive.

She's ignited something inside me. It's not just the sex, or the orgasms. It's something more. Once the pleasure of my orgasm fades, I rest my head on the pillow and watch the smile play across her lips. My heart jumps as we lie in bed together.

When she's in the shower, I put on some eggs and bacon for breakfast. She comes into the tiny kitchen with a towel wrapped around her, inhaling and smiling. I hand her a cup of coffee and she takes a long drink.

"This is the perfect morning," she says. She looks out the window and then back at me. "Listen!"

I listen to the birds singing right outside the window and I watch her look outside. She points at a nearby tree and looks at me with a huge smile on her face. "A nest! There must be babies hatching!"

I nod, flipping the bacon. "They're sparrows," I say. "I've been watching them the past couple of days. They hatched two days ago, and the mom has been busy feeding them ever since."

Mara stares out the window and I smile as I watch her face. You'd think she'd never seen a bird's nest before.

"Even being just a little bit further out, you get so much more wildlife here," she says. "It's way too busy near the hotel. It's nice here."

I nod, dishing up a couple plates of breakfast. Mara tears herself away from the window and smiles.

"This looks amazing," she breathes.

"Between last night and this morning, you've pretty much gotten my full repertoire of cooking," I laugh.

"Well, I'm impressed," she answers. She leans over to me and plants a kiss on my lips. "It smells so good."

We spend the next hour or so just enjoying each other's company. I used to think my cabin would never be big enough for two people, but Mara seems completely at home here. I put my arm around her and kiss her temple as we sit on the couch. She turns to me and kisses my lips before smiling sadly.

"I'd better go," she says. "Any later and people will start wondering where I am."

"I can drive you back," I offer.

"That's okay, I'll walk the back way. It's such a beautiful day."

I nod and kiss her one more time. When she leaves, I watch her walk through the trees in the direction of town, and my heart feels light. I finish the rest of my coffee and put the mug in the sink before heading out to the workshop. I've got sketches for a few items that Mara wants to prototype. Based on the contract she showed me yesterday, I'm going to be incredibly busy for the next couple of months.

I get to work with a smile on my face and a lightness in my heart that I'm not used to. As unlikely as it is, Mara McCoy has brought the joy back to my life.

20

MARA

THE DAYS GO by in a flurry of activity. Renovations begin on the hotel, and I do my best to orchestrate them. I steal any moment I can with Dominic, and the two of us collaborate on the design of the furniture for the hotel.

"Where did you find someone on such short notice?" My mother exclaims as I show her the prototypes for the nightstands. "Furniture makers are usually so busy!"

I shrug, trying to keep my face steady. "I'm just resourceful, I guess."

"You sure are," she breathes. She inspects the nightstands and nods in approval. "These are perfect. Who made them?"

"A small woodworker from Wolf Mountain," I lie. My heart squeezes. I hate lying, even if I know it's for the best. My father looks up from the perfect workmanship of the furniture and studies my face. My palms start to sweat as he stares at me, but finally he looks away and says nothing. I take a deep breath and slip away from the two of them.

I'm glad that they like the designs so far, but I'm not sure how much I'll be able to hide from them. Surely the truth will come out – especially if Dominic and I are spending more and more time together.

I sleep over at his cabin a couple of times a week, and I steal any moment I can to go to his workshop. He'll sneak into my room in the dead of night to sleep next to me for a few hours. I know we should be more careful, or we should just come clean, but everything is too perfect right now to consider it.

He's attentive and loving and funny. I never thought Dominic Clarke could be funny, but he is. I used to think he was the most stoic of the Clarke brothers – the real mountain man. He looks like one! He's huge, taking up most of whatever room he happens to be in. His voice is deep and when he furrows his brows, he looks almost scary.

But when his face softens and that spark appears in his eyes, his true self shines through. That's the Dominic that makes my heart jump.

"There," Dominic says, wiping the last bit of sawdust off the top of the headboard prototype. I take a step back and compare it to the sketch in my hand. I nod.

"Looks good. The arch is much better on this one. You were right about the bevel – it definitely makes it look more expensive."

"It's almost like I know what I'm talking about," he answers with a grin. I elbow him in the ribs and look at the piece of furniture again.

"Do you think you'll be able to make a hundred and four of these? Can't you hire someone to help you?"

"Well, with all this cash you're injecting into my business, I guess I could."

I laugh. "Is that the only reason you keep me around?"

"One of them," he answers with a grin. "I also like to hear you critique my headboard construction."

"We could test out how sturdy it is," I answer as a grin floats onto my lips. He takes a step toward me and I inhale the smell of musk and sawdust.

"I think some testing would be wise. We wouldn't want any of the hotel guests to get injured."

I smile, taking a step toward him. The heat of his body is almost intoxicating. Whenever I'm near him, it's like I'm drunk. All my movements are in slow motion. He steps closer to me and I have to tilt my chin up to keep looking at his face. His chest is twice as broad as mine, and his hands find my waist. Our bodies are so close that I can almost hear his heartbeat. I close my eyes and tilt my chin up toward him, waiting for the kiss that I know is coming.

It never comes, though. Both of us go stiff and jump apart when someone clears their throat at the entrance to the workshop.

"Aiden!" Dominic exclaims. His voice almost comes out as a squeak as he takes another step away from me. I brush the front of my clothes and feel my cheeks burn as I look toward Dominic's younger brother.

He looks exactly as he did when we were kids. My heart starts thumping in my chest and familiar guilt starts curdling in my stomach.

Aiden's eyes swing from Dominic to me and a jolt passes through me. He was my first love. When I was a teenager, I was sure I would marry him. Now, when he looks at me all I see is loathing. It broke my heart to lose him, but now he feels like a stranger.

He takes a step and looks at his brother again.

"Am I interrupting anything?" Aiden grunts with an eyebrow raised.

Dominic shakes his head. "Nah. Just looking at this furniture," he says, taking another step away from me and nodding to the headboard. "How was the honeymoon?"

"Fine," Aiden replies.

I know why he's avoiding my stare. I know it would cause trouble with his brothers, and my parents, and everyone else in town. But still, when Dominic steps away from me it sends a dagger of pain through my heart.

For the past couple weeks, we've been all over each other. He hasn't taken his hands off me. I've gotten to know his body as well as my own. And now, with Aiden looking at us, he's avoiding my eyes and turning away from me.

I nod. "Anyway, it looks good. I'll pick it up to get approval on it tomorrow."

Dominic grunts in response and I look from him to his brother. Neither of them looks at me, and I slip out of the workshop with a lump in my throat. My stomach feels like a rock as I climb into the truck that my parents lent me. It has the familiar 'McCoy Trucking' logo on the side. For the thousandth time since I've gotten back, I curse my last name. I wish I came from a different family. I wish I could choose who I wanted to be with, and I wish everything between the Clarkes and me had never happened.

I wish Dominic and I could stop sneaking around and be together. I wish Aiden didn't look at me like that every time he saw me. I turn my head toward the workshop, and my eyes start to prickle as I think of the two men inside.

One of them I loved when I was a teenager. After the accident and his dad's pneumonia, I was dead to him. When my parents bought out Mr. Clarke's business, it was the beginning of the feud.

Now, the other brother in that workshop holds a special place in my heart as well. I can feel myself falling for him more every day. As much as I try to stop myself, there's nothing I can do about it.

I'm falling in love with the one man who can't be with me.

I'm falling in love with Dominic Clarke.

21

———

DOMINIC

IT'S NOT until the noise of Mara's truck fades down the driveway that Aiden speaks again.

"You're working with the *McCoys*?" he spits.

I sigh and turn back to the headboard. I try to hide the sour expression on my face, and the pain that I felt when I watched Mara walk out. I know I hurt her. I should have told Aiden what was going on. I shouldn't have denied anything.

"I didn't have any other choice."

"Like fuck you didn't," Aiden says again, taking a step toward me. Suddenly, anger starts to bloom in my chest. I look at the outrage on his face and I'm as offended as he is. I take a step toward him and square my shoulders.

"That's pretty fucking hypocritical for you to say," I snap. "You worked for them for years before starting your own garage."

"That was different."

"How?"

He says nothing, just stands in front of me with daggers in his eyes.

"Grow the fuck up, Aiden," I growl, taking another step in his direction. He doesn't back down. "Mara is not the reason that Dad died. She's not the reason that her parents took his business. She's not a bad person."

Aiden snorts and looks at me like I have three heads. "Excuse me? If it's not her fault that Dad died, whose is it?"

I stare at my brother, seeing the fury in his eyes. I've always known that he took Dad's death the hardest, but I had no idea how strongly he still felt about it, even a decade later.

"It was an accident, Aiden," I say a bit more softly. "If Dad had gone to the hospital instead of refusing –"

"If she hadn't fallen in the fucking river, you mean. If *that* hadn't happened then he'd still be here."

"It was an *accident*," I say again. My patience is starting to wear thin. Now that I know Mara – now that I see what kind of heart she has – I feel so guilty about the past ten years. We've shut her out of our lives and out of the town, just because of an accident that happened when we were teens. Aiden bristles in front of me and I know that I won't be able to convince him. "She's not a bad person."

"Well, even if she isn't, her parents are. Have you forgotten that they stole Dad's business when he was on his death bed? They tricked us into signing it over! And now you're *working* for them?"

I can hear the hurt in his voice and my own anger starts to fade. My shoulders slump and I shake my head. How can I make him understand? How could I possibly tell him that I'm falling for *Mara McCoy*, of all people?

All I do is sigh. I shake my head and shrug my shoulders. "I'm sick of this, Aiden," I say. He stares at me with fire in his eyes and I shake my head again. "I'm sick of the fighting, the animosity, and this whole feud! Sure, the McCoys screwed us over. They're opportunistic and cruel, but what does hating them do for *us*?"

His chest is heaving up and down and he stares at me, waiting for me to continue.

I take a deep breath. "Look, you can feel however you want to. You can hate them for the rest of your life, but I'm sick of it."

I turn back toward my workbench and pick up the nearest tool. I just want him to leave. Instead of leaving, he takes a step toward me.

"So are you fucking her now, too?"

I spin toward him and grab his collar. "Watch your fucking mouth," I growl, my face inches from his.

"Or what?"

I've never come so close to hitting my own brother. The anger is boiling inside me and it feels like I'm about to explode. To hear my own brother speaking about Mara like that makes my stomach turn. We're locked together, coiled like tight springs, staring into each other's eyes as both of us wait to see what the other will do. I see nothing in his eyes except aggression and anger. Maybe that's exactly what's in my eyes, too.

I back down first. I throw him back and nod to the door.

"Get the fuck out," I say.

"So you're choosing them, are you? You're choosing money and pussy over your own family?"

"Fuck you, Aiden. Get off your high horse. You'd still be working for the McCoys if you hadn't married a rich city girl. You think you started that business by yourself, do you?"

Aiden lunges for me, and I almost stumble backward before catching his forearm in my hand before he can hit me. We grapple with each other, straining against the workbench and pushing each other until I'm able to get him off me. I push him back and he stumbles, brushing himself off and standing up straighter. There's fire in his eyes and the tension is thick between us. He takes another step forward, lifting his fists up.

"Aiden," I say. I try to keep my voice calm but I see him bristle.

He lunges toward me again, and this time I'm not able to lift my arm in time to block him. I deflect his punch, but his fist connects with my lip in an explosion of pain. I grunt and stumble back, falling over against the new headboard. It cracks down the middle with a loud pop and I grunt again. Aiden stands in front of me and snarls.

"You've changed, Dominic," he says. He throws me one more look of pure venom and then turns toward the door. I hear his truck rumble to life and speed down the road.

I slump down onto the floor and put my head in my hands. I touch my finger to my lip and feel it swelling up already. There's bright red blood on my fingers when I pull them away. I sigh, closing my eyes and leaning my head against the ruined headboard.

What have I done? What am I doing?

My own brother thinks I'm a traitor. I'm trying to move on from the past, but it's causing even more issues with my family. I'm trying to make my business work, but it will just create friction in the town.

What happens when everyone else finds out? What happens when people find out that I'm not only working for the McCoys, but I'm also sleeping with Mara? What happens when the *McCoys* find out I'm working for them! And that I'm sleeping with their daughter!

I let out a sigh and comb my hair back with my fingers. I have no idea what I'm supposed to do. It feels like the right thing to do would be to break it off with Mara and back out of the contract. But what if that's not the right thing to do? That's just what's expected of me. Why are we hanging on to this anger and hatred if it's just out of *habit*?

The look on Aiden's face said more than habit though. The way he lunged at me said more than expectation. He's never hit me like that before. I'm not sure it's worth it. Should I destroy my relationship with my brother over this contract – over Mara?

I lean back against the new headboard and let out a sigh. Everything feels heavy. My limbs feel like they're made of lead and my chest feels like it's sunken in.

I need to get out of this workshop. I can't look at any of this today.

22

MARA

IT's hard for me to focus on work. I don't know what to think. I'm in the small office at the front of the hotel, staring at my computer screen. Every time I look at my sketches, all I see is gibberish. It's like my eyes can't focus on anything long enough to make any sense of it. I squint at my computer screen one more time before giving up and putting my head in my hands.

I keep seeing the look on Aiden's face when he walked into the workshop – it's the same look that he's given me ever since his dad died. I've always known that this would be an issue, but I didn't know that it would sting this much. I've gotten used to Dominic seeing me for me, but Aiden still looks at me with the same disgust and resentment.

Dominic and I have been ignoring the obvious – that sneaking around isn't going to last. Our relationship is pretty much universally frowned upon.

Does Aiden know we're seeing each other? What did he see when he walked in on us?

Familiar, bitter guilt starts growing inside me when I think of Aiden. I wish I could make him understand that I have no hard feelings toward him. I wish I could just be open with him and tell him how happy I am that he's found a woman he loves, and how happy I am that his new business is doing well. I wish he'd look me in the eye long enough to see how much I mean it when I say I'm sorry.

As much as I tell myself that Mr. Clarke didn't die because of me, it's hard to believe it. I've carried that weight on my shoulders for over ten years, and all I want is to get rid of it. I want to see something other than hatred in Aiden's and his brothers' eyes.

For the past couple weeks, I've finally felt like I can breathe. Dominic sees me for who I am. He doesn't see the accident when he looks at me. I've never felt like he blames me for his father's death. I've been able to talk about it for the first time without feeling like I had to apologize.

I slump on my desk chair and look at the mess of drawings and paperwork in front of me. The renovations are in full swing and I have a thousand and one things to do – but right now all I can think about is Dominic avoiding my gaze and Aiden staring at me with daggers in his eyes.

I'm not sure which one hurt more.

My eyes are prickling and my heart is beating faster than normal as I lean back in my chair. I bring my hands up to my face, trying to stop the tears from pouring out of my eyes. With a deep, raking breath, I look at the ceiling and shake my head.

I look at my phone and pick it up, running my fingers over the screen. Should I call Dominic? Should I go see him?

Even though I knew this would happen, I still don't know how to react. I don't know if I should ignore it and give him space, and hope it'll all go away. I don't know if anything has changed. We always knew that his brothers, and Aiden especially, wouldn't be happy about seeing us together. I've always known Aiden despises me.

I put my phone down with a sigh. I wouldn't even know

what to say to him. I can't ask him to take our relationship public. Is it even a relationship? We've been sleeping together for the past couple weeks. He makes me feel like I'm floating, but is it just sex? Do I mean as much to him as he means to me?

I blow the air out of my nostrils and shake my head. My mind is fucking *melted*. I need to just let this be. Dominic needs time to think, just like I do. I push my chair back and stretch my arms up overhead. I let out a noise and shake my head back and forth.

I'm not being productive. I need some air. Stalking out of the office, I make my way to the back of the hotel toward my bedroom. I pass the kitchen and the staff room on my way to the very back, finally opening the familiar door in the back corner. When I close the door behind me, I lean back against it and close my eyes.

This room feels like my sanctuary. It's quieter than the front of the hotel, and it's always been the place I come to be alone and think. I take a deep breath and lean back against the door, closing my eyes and trying to calm my heartbeat.

I jump at the sound of a knock on the back door. I look up, frowning. There's only one person that uses that door these days.

Dominic.

I cross the room in a few steps and rip the door open. My jaw drops when I see him. His clothes are disheveled and his hair is all over the place. His lip is swollen and bloody, with a thin, red line of blood dripping toward his chin.

"Dominic!" I exclaim. I usher him inside and sit him down on the bed. I take his chin in my hand. "What happened? Are you okay?"

"I'm fine," he says.

"Wait here."

I rush out the door toward the front of the hotel, finding the nearest First Aid kit. I grab some ice and come back with an armful of bandages. Dominic is still sitting on my bed. He's not moving, only staring out the window in a daze.

I stand in front of him and start cleaning his lip before icing it. I wipe the water that drips down from the ice cube and run my fingers through his hair. I kiss his temple and blink back tears. Dominic closes his eyes and groans in satisfaction as I rub his scalp.

"What happened?" I whisper. "Oh, Dominic, I'm so sorry."

He opens his eyes and looks directly at me. "Stop apologizing," he growls. His eyes are clear and his voice is forceful, so all I do is nod. "Mara," he continues. "Do you hear me? You did nothing wrong."

A lump forms in my throat and my eyes start to blur. I nod my head and take the ice cube away from his lip. I clean the wound one more time and get to work putting a small bandage over the cut. Dominic stares at me while I work, and I try my best to avoid his gaze.

His hands trail up my legs and rest on my thighs. I lean into his touch and take a deep breath, moving my hands to his shoulders and leaning my forehead against his. When I pull away, there are tears in my eyes.

"I never wanted this to happen, Dominic. I don't want to cause even more trouble in your family. It's not worth it."

"Don't tell me what's worth it or not," he says. "I'll decide that for myself."

He stares straight at me and I put my hands on either side of his face. I bring my lips to his forehead and kiss him tenderly, pressing my lips against his skin. He wraps his arms around my waist and pulls me closer. We stay like that for a few moments until I pull away and look at him with my eyes full of tears. I try to smile.

"I'd kiss you right now, but with that lip..."

Dominic grins and grabs my waist, flipping me over beside

him onto the bed. He shifts his body around so that he's on top of me, leaning his weight on his elbow. He runs his finger down my cheek and lays his lips against mine. When he pulls away, he looks into my eyes and smiles.

"I don't care about the lip," he whispers. "I only care about you."

23

DOMINIC

SEEING the smile light up Mara's face feels like a healing balm on my heart. My lip is throbbing, but I don't feel any pain. She's smiling at me and running her fingers along the side of my head. I groan before dipping my head down to lay a soft kiss on her lips.

It feels right to be here with her. It feels good. I know that Aiden disapproves. I know her parents wouldn't approve if they knew we were seeing each other. I know Ethan might not understand, but I can't help it. After Aiden left, all I wanted to do was make sure she was okay.

I'm lying on top of her on the bed, framing her face with my forearms as I lean on my elbows. She smiles at me and I shake my head.

"You're so beautiful, Mara. You know that?"

"Stop it," she says. Her cheeks redden the tiniest bit, and my smile widens. My lip aches as the swollen skin stretches, but it doesn't stop me from smiling.

"I mean it." I take a deep breath and stare into her eyes. "I didn't mean to hurt you, back there – when Aiden showed up. It caught me by surprise and I didn't know how to react."

She tilts her head to the side and runs her fingers up the side of my body. "I get it," she responds. "I didn't know how to react either."

I press my lips against hers as she lifts my shirt up and runs her hands along the skin on my back. I groan and press my body into hers. When I pull away, I can already see the question in her eyes.

"Dominic," she starts. She stares at me for a second before continuing: "What are we doing? What is this? Where does it go from here?"

"Why does it need to go anywhere?" I ask, and I immediately know it was the wrong thing to say. She looks at me and frowns. "No, I didn't mean it like that. I mean…" My voice trails off.

"You mean that this is as far as it can go between us." she finishes softly. Her voice is calm. I force myself to look at her again and see the hurt in her eyes. My voice is gone and I don't know how to respond. I shake my head.

"No, that's not what I meant."

"So what did you mean?"

I take a deep breath and roll onto my back. My legs are hanging off the edge of the bed, and Mara turns toward me. She rests her head on her hand as she lies on her side, waiting for me to answer.

"I don't know how this is going to work between us, Mara. You make me feel…" I pause. "I don't know. You make me feel *alive*. It's like I've been in a daze for years. The past couple of weeks I've actually been seeing clearly."

I look at her but she doesn't respond, so I take a deep breath and keep going.

"I just…" I shake my head. "I don't know how Aiden would ever come to terms with it."

"*It* being us?"

"Yeah."

She nods, staring off at a point behind me. Her eyes look like they're glazed over, and I run my fingers along her jaw to pull her back to me.

"I'll figure it out, Mara," I whisper. "I came here, didn't I? I came straight to you once he left."

I can see her swallow as she nods. I pull her down toward me and she melts into me, pressing her lips against mine.

This time, when we make love, I'm gentle with her. She's trembling and she feels as fragile as a porcelain doll. I run my hands over her body and kiss her with soft lips. I kiss her until her body relaxes into the bed and then I kiss her some more. I hold her against me, wrapping my arms around her body and keeping her close. Her heart beats against my chest and I catch her lips between mine once more.

She gives herself to me, and I give myself to her. Our bodies meld together until passion consumes us and she finally relaxes. I kiss her again and again, hoping that she can feel what I feel for her. When she comes, she puts her hands on either side of my face and looks into my eyes. I can see her passion, her desire, her affection.

When we're both spent and panting, I run my fingers up and down her spine. She shivers and moans gently before turning her head toward me on the pillow.

"I don't want to stop seeing you," she says. Her voice is so soft and quiet, but it rings in my ears. I nod as my heart grows in my chest. I bring my forehead to hers and kiss her tenderly.

"I don't want to stop seeing you either, Mara. Not even a little bit."

The corners of her mouth lift ever so slightly and I kiss her again. My heart is thumping, and I feel like something between us has changed. It's almost like the spell we've been under for the past two weeks is starting to crack. I don't know if it's the start of something special, or the beginning of the end.

I hope it's the start of something special. I wrap my arms around her and pull her into me. She rests her head against my chest and sighs as I keep running my fingers up and down her spine. I'm only just getting to know her, and I'm not ready to let her go.

As she curls her fingers and presses herself into me, I know that I can't let her go. It doesn't matter what my brothers think, or what the town thinks, or what her parents think. She's shown me more affection and passion and laughter in the past few weeks than I've known for the past ten *years*. She's showing me a new side of myself that I didn't even know existed.

No, I'm not ready to let her go. I'll take a thousand swollen lips from Aiden and a million disapproving stares just to lie next to her at night, and wake up next to her in the morning.

24

MARA

WHEN DOMINIC LEAVES, I'm calm. I'm able to head back to my desk and get some work done until it's completely dark outside and my eyes are starting to shut on their own. I close my computer down and jump when there's a knock on the door frame.

I turn to see my father leaning in the opening of the door.

"Hey, Mara," he says. "You're working late today."

"Lots to do," I respond, sweeping my eyes over my desk to make sure there's no sign of Dominic. "You guys are quite the slave drivers."

My dad chuckles and pulls up a chair, leaning on his knees as he groans to sit down. He takes a deep breath and looks at me. I turn in my chair to face him and wait for him to speak. Ever since I got back, I've been keeping my distance from my parents. Most days, I don't know what to say to them anymore.

"Mara, you know I'm proud of you, right? The work that you've been doing on the hotel has been exceptional."

I nod my head, not trusting my voice.

"I'm sorry about your engagement. I thought Vincent was a good one."

My eyes narrow as I stare at my father. Is this another mind game? Why would he say that when the whole reason Vincent agreed to marry me was some fucked-up business transaction?

"Right," I finally respond. "Was that before or after you decided to use me as a bargaining chip to build the new hotel?"

My dad's eyebrows shoot up and he puts his hands on the chair's armrests. "Is that what you think?"

"Isn't that what happened?" I spit. Suddenly, all the emotion from the past weeks and months is bubbling up inside me. My failed engagement, the feelings of betrayal and mistrust, the peace that I've found with Dominic – it's all coming to a head.

He shakes his head and makes a noise. "No, no. Mara, that's not what happened. I would never use you like that."

"Wouldn't you? Isn't that what you were doing with Aiden before Mr. Clarke died? And then you didn't need me anymore once you acquired the trucking business, so you traded me to the next highest bidder instead."

I can hear the venom in my voice and I don't care. My father stares at me as if I'm a stranger, and I stare right back at him. We stay there, motionless. He shakes his head from side to side.

"No, Mara. I never did that. I didn't even want the trucking business. It was your mother who –"

He stops, looking out toward the hallway and back at me. His mouth drops open and then closes again. He stares at the ground for a few moments and then shakes his head.

"No. That's not what happened."

"Isn't it? Why else did Vincent break up with me the minute the construction of the new hotel was abandoned? Why else did you encourage me to date Aiden and then turn your back on him the moment his father died?"

My father pushes himself up to stand and shakes his head. "Mara..."

"Just go, Dad. I've got lots of work to do. I don't even know why I'm doing this for you, after everything you've put me through. I thought maybe I could..." *Atone. Make it up to the Clarke brothers. Do something for myself.*

I turn my back on my father and start shuffling some papers. I hear him walk out the door and down the hallway. My heart squeezes in my chest. My eyes are prickling but I don't let myself cry.

It felt good to say it out loud. It felt good to tell him that I knew about their plans – that I wasn't going to get played again. It felt good to stand up for myself for once. I run my fingers through my hair and exhale.

I close my eyes and lean back in my chair.

What am I doing here? Why am I here?

I could be anywhere. I didn't need to come back here after Vincent and I broke up. I could have gone to LA, or New York, or anywhere in between. I could have moved to Paris!

Instead, I chose Lang Creek. I *chose* to start working for my parents. I *chose* to put myself in this position.

Why?

The question swirls around my mind and I rub my temples. Am I some sort of masochist? I willingly came back here when I knew that they were the ones who put me in that situation with Vincent in the first place.

I finally open my eyes and see one of the first sketches I did. I see Dominic's changes, and the precise pencil marks that he made to alter the drawings. I pick it up and look at our joint design, and my heart starts to beat a little bit faster.

I have my answer.

I'm here because of *him*. Maybe I didn't know it when I came back, but now I know why I've stayed. I know why I proposed the hotel renovations, and why I'm doing all this work.

I'm doing it to spend time with Dominic. Maybe it's me making amends for the accident that led to Mr. Clarke's death. Or maybe – just maybe – I've started falling for Dominic. Maybe I've found someone that finally understands and accepts me.

Maybe...

...I'm in *love*.

I stare at the sketch until the lines start to blur together. Finally, I drop the sheet and push myself off my chair. I take a slow walk to the back of the building and push my bedroom door open. My room is cold and dark, and I collapse into bed.

I'm in love with Dominic Clarke.

The words play on repeat over, and over, and over in my mind. I don't understand how it has happened. I don't understand why it's happened, but it has.

I'm in love.

I stare at the ceiling and feel my heart beating against my ribcage. Now that I've admitted it to myself, it seems so much bigger and more real than it did before.

If this is love – *real* love, I mean – if this is love, then it's worth fighting for. It's worth putting up with Aiden's animosity, and my parents' disapproval. It's worth admitting to the whole town that I want to be with Dominic.

If this is love, then I sure as hell hope Dominic feels the same way. I don't think I can take another heartbreak. I'm letting myself fall for Dominic...

...if it ends badly then I'm not sure I'll ever be the same.

25

DOMINIC

WHEN I LEAVE Mara's room, I feel better. My lip is throbbing but I hardly feel it. All I can think of is Mara's skin, her smell, her smile.

It feels so good to be with her, it can't possibly be wrong. I start walking back toward my place and then pause before turning around and walking the other direction. Before long, I'm outside my brother Ethan's house.

He opens the door after a couple of knocks.

"What happened to you?" He asks, eyebrows raised as he looks at my lip.

"Aiden," I respond. Ethan's eyebrows stay up, but he just nods in response.

"I see."

He steps aside and I walk into his house. I collapse onto the sofa and Ethan grabs me a beer. I take it and nod in thanks.

"So why did Aiden do that to your face?" He asks, taking a seat in the chair opposite me. "What did you do?"

I take a sip of beer and glance at my little brother. "It's my fault, is it?"

Ethan grins. "You must have done something."

"I took a job from the McCoys."

Ethan's mouth drops open and he nods slowly. "Ah," he says. "I see. The renovations."

"Aiden walked in on Mara and me discussing one of the pieces. He... wasn't happy to see her."

"Is 'discussing one of the pieces' a euphemism for something? I remember the way she looked at you when we were at the bar a couple of weeks ago."

I lift an eyebrow and shake my head. "It is *not* a euphemism," I answer. *But it might as well be.*

Ethan chuckles. "Fair enough."

"I don't get why he's so mad at her. She's actually a really nice person, you know. Did you know that she paid for her schooling on her own? I always thought she got that degree with the money from Dad's company, but she worked through college and paid it herself. She started her own consulting business online. She's incredible."

Ethan takes a sip of beer and narrows his eyes. I can feel my cheeks start to burn as he studies my face, but I keep my eyes steady on his. He nods slowly.

"No, I didn't know that," he finally answers.

I take a big gulp of beer and lean back in the sofa. I sigh, looking up at the ceiling.

"I'm sick of this."

"Sick of what?"

"Sick of all this drama over nothing!" I exclaim.

Ethan makes a noise. "Dad dying is nothing? The McCoys taking advantage of us when he was in the hospital is nothing?"

I look at my little brother and see the same indignation in his face as I saw in Aiden's. It's not as strong, but it's there. Doubt starts to curl deep inside me. What if they're right to be mad?

"It's not nothing," I say. "It's just... Wouldn't it be easier to forgive? Mara didn't do anything wrong. Why do we hate her?"

"We don't hate her. We just don't associate with her family."

I look at Ethan and try to figure out what he's thinking. His face is stone still and I sigh, shaking my head.

"So you think I deserve this?" I ask, pointing to my lip.

Ethan's lips start to curl into a grin. He shrugs. "I wouldn't say that. I wouldn't say you *don't* deserve it, but I wouldn't say you do."

"What's that supposed to mean?"

"I can see both sides."

I snort and shake my head, bringing the beer bottle to my lips again. Ethan has always been great at speaking in riddles. Finally, I put the beer down and look at my brother. I'm practically pleading with my eyes before I start to speak.

"Am I wrong here, Ethan? Should I not have taken this job?"

"Well," he says, pausing to take a sip. "That depends. It's a bit hypocritical of Aiden to say that, considering he worked for them for years."

"That's what I said!" I exclaim.

Ethan laughs. "And how did that go over?"

"He punched me in the face," I answer with a grin. Ethan laughs again and shakes his head.

"Look," he says. "I don't know what the right thing to do is. Work is work, and you needed the job. Sounds like it's a big one, so no one can fault you for taking it. It's just money, it's not like you're banging Mara or anything."

My throat tightens and I try to swallow. I avert my eyes and nod as he speaks. Ethan pauses, and I can feel his eyes boring into me.

"Dominic," he says. I drag my eyes up to his and try to keep my face steady.

"Yeah?"

"You're not banging Mara, are you?"

"Well, I..." My shoulders slump and I shrug at my brother. His jaw drops and he shakes his head. He leans back in his chair and brings his beer bottle to his lips. After he drinks, he looks at me again and shakes his head some more.

"Dom," he says.

I shrug. "I don't know how it happened!"

"What, you slipped and accidentally had sex? What do you mean you 'don't know how it happened?'"

"I just mean…" My voice trails off and I look at my brother. All I can do is shrug and shake my head. Finally, a grin starts to appear on his face and his shoulders start to shake. I can feel the laughter bubbling up through my stomach and pretty soon the two of us are doubled over with laughter.

Tears are streaming down my cheeks as I laugh, and laugh, and laugh. Ethan slaps his knee. His face scrunches as he laughs and he throws his head back.

Finally, the two of us quiet down and Ethan shakes his head. I take a deep breath.

"Dom," Ethan says. "*What* are you doing?"

"I'm not sure," I respond, staring into my beer bottle.

"You're playing with fire."

"I'm good at that, apparently," I shoot back. Ethan laughs again and nods.

"True."

I take a deep breath and look at my little brother. It should be me counseling him, not the other way around. I'm almost five years older than him. He stares at me and nods his chin down once before speaking again.

"Do you care about her?"

My throat closes again and my heart thumps in my chest. Ethan's face is completely serious, and I drop my eyes to my beer bottle again. I peel the label off with my fingernail as I chew on his question.

I know the answer.

Of course I care about her. I'm crazy about her. It's never felt this good to be with a woman. I've never met anyone as funny or driven or clever as she is. But how can I say that to Ethan? How can I admit it out loud, when I know that he blames her for Dad's death? Finally, I lift my eyes back up to him and nod.

"Yeah," I croak. "I do."

Ethan takes a deep breath and shrugs.

"Then you're fucked," he says.

I snort and chuckle as I shake my head. "Completely."

26

MARA

Something has changed. I can feel it, even though everything on the surface seems the same. Dominic leaves a bit earlier in the morning, before the sun comes up. He doesn't come into town at all, and I think he's avoiding me in public.

When it's just the two of us, he's just as affectionate as he was a couple of days ago. His hands seem to know my body and he touches me with a tenderness that's surprising from a man his size.

But still, something's changed.

The renovations are about halfway through, with the lobby and dining hall finished and about half the rooms under way. Dominic has been able to deliver all his pieces on time, and they've gotten rave reviews from everyone who's seen them.

"Mara, there you are!" My mother calls out as she comes down the hallway. "I have a surprise for you in the office!"

I glance over. "Okay, I'll be right there. I just want to make sure this furniture goes to the right place."

"When are you going to tell me the name of this furniture maker?" my mother exclaims as another perfect set of night-stands is carried through the door. "His work is exceptional."

I smile and shake my head. "Maybe never."

She clicks her tongue and gives me a sideways glance.

"I can tell you who made those," a voice calls out behind me. A shiver runs down my spine and I already know who the voice belongs to. I'd recognize that voice anywhere. I turn around and my heart sinks like a stone.

"Aiden," I say.

"What are *you* doing here?" my mother snarls.

"That's not the warm greeting you give all your other guests, I hope," he shoots, glancing at my mother. In a second, his eyes are back on me. My heart is thumping against my ribcage, and I open and close my mouth.

"Why are you... Can I help you with anything?"

"I just wanted to make sure we were all on the same page. And from what I can tell," he says, nodding to my mother. "You've kept your parents in the dark."

"What are you talking about? Mara, what is he talking about?" My mother squeals. I ignore her, keeping my eyes trained on Aiden.

"Aiden..." I start, trying to keep my voice calm.

I can see the fire in his eyes. He's angry. He's as angry as I've ever seen him. His broad body is taking up the entire doorway, and his arms are hanging by his sides as he opens and closes his fists. He looks like he's trembling, and I have no idea what he's going to do.

"Mara," he replies through gritted teeth.

When he says my name, I try to suppress a shiver. There was a time when I loved hearing my name on his tongue, when I was drunk in teenage love. Now, it sounds bitter when he says it. He takes a step forward and opens his mouth again.

"Aiden!" A voice calls out from behind him. My heart lifts as I recognize Dominic. He appears behind Aiden and clamps a hand on his shoulder. "Aiden!"

Aiden shrugs the hand off and turns around. "Get your fucking hands off me!"

Ethan, the youngest of the three, appears in the doorway as well. "Come on, Aiden. Don't do this."

"Don't do *what*!" My mother screeches. I put a hand on her forearm and can feel her trembling. "Get out of here! All three of you!"

I put a bit of pressure on her arm to keep her from stepping forward. She's shaking.

The three brothers pay her no attention. There are unspoken words between them, and after a few tense moments, Aiden huffs and spins around, stalking back down the street. I watch him get into his truck and speed off down the road. Dominic and Ethan look at each other, and then back toward me and my mother.

"Sorry about that," Dominic grunts, looking at the ground between us.

Look me in the eye! I want to scream. *Look at me!*

"What's going on?" My mother asks to no one in particular. "Tell me!"

Ethan looks up at me, and I know he knows about me and Dominic. He glances at Dominic who lifts his eyes up to me. I look at the two brothers and glance down the road toward where the third Clarke brother just disappeared. I glance at my mother and take a deep breath.

"Mom," I start, "Dominic is the one who has been making the new furniture."

I think she might faint. She stumbles backward and clutches her heart as I try to keep her steady. Ethan rushes forward, trying to help but she swats him away.

"*WHAT!*" She finally yells. "What did you just say?"

I take a deep breath and glance at Dominic. He finally lifts his eyes up to mine and I see the pain inside him. It's killing him to be in the middle of this.

The guilt coiled deep inside me starts to wake up.

This is all my fault.

That look on his face – the pain, the discomfort, the hurt – it's my fault. I should never have asked him to make this furniture for us. I should never have gotten involved with him. I've once again caused trouble for his family and dragged him into a situation that he wants no part of.

I turn to my mother and take a deep breath. "He's the best there is, Mom."

"Do you think I *care*?" She exclaims. She looks at me, wide-eyed, until my shoulders slump. "Mara! Inside. Now!"

She stalks off toward the office and I watch her go before turning to the brothers. I take a step toward Dominic and try to put my hand on his arm but he steps away from me.

I drop my hand and feel a hot knife pass through my heart as he looks away from me. I glance at Ethan, who looks at his brother and then at me.

"I'm sorry," I say.

Dominic finally looks at me and shakes his head. "I should never have gotten involved with you. I knew it would be trouble, and here we are. This?" he moves his finger from me back to himself. "This was a mistake."

My chest feels hollow. My eyes are starting to blur as his words sink in. I watch him turn around and get into Ethan's waiting truck. Ethan glances at me and follows his brother without saying a word. When they drive off, they take the air out of my lungs and the light from my eyes. They turn the corner and drive out of view as the first tear spills over my cheek.

I turn around and look down the hallway where my mother disappeared. I take a deep breath and start the long walk over to the office, preparing myself for the worst.

This was a mistake.

His words are ringing in my ears and I brush the hot tears

from my eyes. I try to compose myself in the few seconds before I have to face my mother. Somehow, I'll have to hide the fact that my heart is shattered into a million pieces.

I stumble back to my room and sit on my bed in a daze.

I'm not sure how much time goes by. Minutes? Hours? I finally lift myself up and take a deep breath. I make the long walk back toward the office. My feet feel heavy, and I struggle to keep my shoulders back. My chest is hollow and I feel completely empty.

When I turn the corner into the office, my heart somehow drops further down into my stomach. I stop in my tracks and open my mouth in shock as I look at the visitor in the office.

This must be the 'surprise' that my mother was talking about.

My mother's furious face is staring at me. Beside her, sitting in my desk chair, is my smug, suave ex-fiancé.

"Vincent? What are you doing here?" I exclaim.

My voice comes out as a squeak and I stare from him to my mother in shock.

"Hello, Mara," he says as a smirk spreads over his face. "It's nice to see you too."

27

DOMINIC

ETHAN and I drive in silence. After a few long moments, he takes a deep breath.

"Don't," I say before he can speak. "Please, Ethan. I don't want to talk about it."

I see Ethan nod out of the corner of my eye and I keep staring out the window. I wish I wasn't putting him in this position, but I couldn't help myself. Something about Mara draws me to her. She's irresistible.

Plus, I needed the work.

Why should I stay away from Mara based on some old feud from 10 years ago! I don't have any hard feelings for her.

When we get to the edge of town, instead of turning down the long gravel road to my house, Ethan continues straight. I glance over at him.

"Where are we going?"

"We're going to Aiden's," he replies. His tone of voice leaves no room for discussion. My heart starts thumping a bit harder, and I stare at the trees and mountains going by as we drive down the road.

My muscles tense as we get closer to the winding road that

will take us up the mountain to Aiden's cabin. The sky seems darker all of a sudden. The drive seems to take forever.

Finally, the tension is too much for me. I turn to Ethan.

"What do you expect me to say to him? I'm pretty sure the contract is finished now. You saw Mrs. McCoy."

"I expect you to *talk* to him."

I sigh and shake my head. "Ethan, what kind of good is *talking* going to do? What do you want me to say?"

Ethan glances over at me and a pang passes through my chest. His eyes soften and he looks back toward the road. We turn off on the familiar gravel road that will take us to Aiden's. Instead of driving up, Ethan pulls over on the shoulder and turns to me.

"I agree with you," he starts. He stares at me and I see my father's wisdom in his eyes. He takes a deep breath and pauses.

"But...?" I urge him to continue.

"But is it worth it?" There's something different in the way that he's looking at me. I see something in him that I haven't seen since we were teenagers, standing around our father's deathbed. I see the sadness and loneliness that's been curled deep inside all of us for the past ten years.

I look away from him and stare out the windscreen. The pine trees are swaying gently. The sun is shining and big puffy white clouds are floating through the sky. It's a picture-perfect day, but it feels like the weather is laughing at me.

I shrug. "I don't know, Ethan. I just can't bring myself to be mad at her."

Ethan nods. We sit in silence, considering each other's words for a few minutes. After a pause, Ethan puts the car in gear again and starts the slow, winding drive up the mountain.

We crawl upwards, until finally the trees clear and I see the house that we grew up in. Aiden renovated it and moved into it with his new wife. The cabin that he lived in for almost ten years has been converted into a workshop.

Ethan glances at me and kills the engine. We step out of his car and make our way toward the house. Our shoes crunch on the gravel. A bird sings in a nearby tree, but otherwise the forest is completely silent.

As I put my foot on the first step up to the porch, the front door swings open. Aiden's dark face greets us without a word. I pause, not knowing what to say to him. He glances from me to Ethan and his brows knit together. Finally, he swings the door open and nods for us to come in.

Without a word, he leads us to the kitchen at the back of the house. I glance around, feeling like a stranger in my childhood home. He's made so many changes that it might as well be a different house. We get to the kitchen and Aiden leans against the counter. There's a big oak table in front of us, and Aiden motions to it.

"You know how I've been looking through Dad's old stuff in the attic?"

I grunt in response, looking at the papers on the table. I take a step closer, frowning. They look like letters. I recognize my father's handwriting on a couple of them, but most of them are unfamiliar. I pick one up, scanning it quickly and settling my eyes on the name at the bottom.

My eyebrows shoot upwards and I glance at Aiden. Ethan is staring at me, gauging my reaction. My mouth goes dry and my tongue feels almost too big for my mouth. I try to swallow and look at the letter again. I clear my throat.

"This is a love letter," I finally say. "Addressed to Dad."

Aiden nods. "It's from Margaret McCoy. There are dozens like it."

I glance at the table, picking up another letter at random. My heart is thumping against my chest and I frown again. I shake my head, then stare at the letters before glancing back at my brothers.

"I don't get it. Were they having an affair? Was this after Mom died?"

Ethan and Aiden glance at each other. Ethan answers first.

"We're not sure. There aren't any letters that Dad wrote. The last one is here," he says, picking a crumpled paper out of the stack. "It's dated right after the accident."

I take the paper from my brother and frown. "You knew about this?" I ask Ethan.

"I just found these a couple days ago," Aiden responds. "I showed Ethan yesterday."

"Were you planning on telling me?" I ask, suddenly angry at being left in the dark. Ethan nods.

"Of course. With you and Mara, and your contract with the McCoys…" His voice trails off, and I frown.

"I don't get it. Why would I care about this? It's ten years ago."

"Just read it," Aiden grunts. I look back at the crumpled paper and frown as I try to make out the faded writing.

MY DARLING CALVIN,

I'VE SPENT the last two days in agony, blaming myself for what happened at the river. I shouldn't have suggested going down to the river, but I couldn't bear to be apart from you for another day. Being near you is like a soothing balm on my soul. Stealing glances your way as our children played together is the sweetest joy.

Your last letter has shattered my heart. Knowing you want nothing to do with me is tearing me apart. You saved my daughter's life, and I can never thank you enough. And now, I just want to be by your side for the rest of time.

Calvin, please, my Calvin. Don't walk away from me.

· · ·

I READ the letter three times and finally look up at my brothers. I shake my head.

"I don't get it."

"He broke up with her after the accident, I guess," Ethan says. "That's what I figure, anyway."

"And then he got sick," I say, looking back at the crumpled piece of paper.

"And Margaret McCoy bought out Dad's company from underneath us," Aiden replies. I glance up at his face, and I see a torrent of emotions passing over it. I pull up a chair and sit down, putting my head in my hand, staring at the letter.

"So, this whole thing...?" I breathe. "This whole *feud*, or whatever it is... it's *revenge*? For Dad breaking up with her? She cheated on Tim that whole time?"

I glance up at my brothers and they shrug in unison.

"That's what I can figure out," Ethan says.

"That's why Margaret can't stand us," I breathe. The realization hits me like a tidal wave. My eyes widen and I look at the dozens and dozens of letters on the table.

"She's going to fuck you over," Aiden says. He sighs, rubbing his forehead with his hand. "Even if Mara cares about you. Even if you care about her," he says. "Margaret McCoy will fuck you over."

I try to make sense of everything. I try to understand what this changes – if it changes anything. Margaret was cheating on her husband with our *dad*. He broke it off with her, and then he died – and she bought his business out from under us. She hasn't been able to stand us since.

"Mara told me that her parents used her to do the deal with the luxury hotel. They married her off to the highest bidder, basically," I say.

"Sounds about right," Aiden replies bitterly. He sighs. "Look, Dominic. I don't care about you and Mara. I thought I did, but I don't. I dated her when I was seventeen." He sighs, tilting his head back and looking at the ceiling. He shakes his head and my heart races as he opens his mouth to speak.

"All this," he says, nodding to the table. "It runs a lot deeper than we ever knew."

"I don't know if you should get involved with them," Ethan finishes. I stare at my brothers and then at the letters. My shoulders slump. Mara's face appears in my mind. I see her on my pillow, with her hair around her head like a halo, and the sweetest smile on her lips. I see the sunlight streaming through the window onto her perfect body, and I feel the happiness flood my veins when I think of waking up next to her. I glance at the crumpled letter in my hand, and I take a deep breath.

"I don't know what to think," I finally reply.

28

MARA

"WHAT ARE YOU DOING HERE? What is *he* doing here?" I look from Vincent to my mother and frown. This feels wrong. It feels all wrong. Alarm bells are going off in my mind and I try to make sense of what I'm seeing.

This is the man that didn't even say goodbye to me. This is the man who sent his personal assistant to help his ex-fiancée move out of his mansion.

Vincent gets up and takes a step toward me. I take a step back and put up my hand.

"Mara," he croons. "Come on, babe."

"Don't call me babe. I'm not your babe."

His face softens as a hint of hesitation pierces my heart. Memories pass through my mind like a flash – all the times we had candlelit dinners and romantic walks. All the vacations and presents he got me.

I look at him again and frown.

It was all fake. I've felt more affection in a few weeks with Dominic than I did in three years with him. He was just buying me, like he buys everyone and everything around him.

"What are you doing here?"

"Mara, darling," my mother interjects. "Vincent reached out to me. He realizes what a mistake he's made and wanted to come back. He wanted to make it up to you in person."

I swing my eyes over to my mother and frown. "Excuse me?"

"I miss you," Vincent says. I look back at him and take a step back as he takes another step toward me. My heart is beating furiously and my head is screaming *run*. My feet stay rooted in place and all I can do is look at the man who played me for a fool.

"Why are you here?" I croak.

"I needed to see you," he says gently. My breath is shallow and my heart is thumping. This feels wrong. It all feels wrong.

Dominic is gone. My mother is furious. Vincent is here.

This is all wrong.

This isn't how this was supposed to happen. I don't understand what's happening. Does he care about me? Was I wrong about being used?

My father clears his throat behind me and I jump. I turn to him, eyes wide as I stare at the three of them.

"Mara," he says, putting his hand on my arm. I jump. "Mara, Vincent reached out to your mother and we invited him to come here."

I shake my head back and forth as the words catch in my throat. I don't know what to say. The betrayal I felt when I came back here is bubbling up inside me. I don't know where to turn. I don't know where to go.

Dominic doesn't want to see me, and my parents only think of themselves. The man who used me to advance his business is standing right in front of me, turning on his charm like a faucet.

I'm alone.

Vincent takes a step toward me and this time I don't back up. He motions to the door and the side of his mouth curls into a gentle smile.

"Walk and talk with me?"

I'm almost suffocating in this room, and I can't think. I just nod and let him guide me back in the direction I came in from, and then out the hotel's front door. The sunlight outside is almost blinding. I'm walking in a daze, vaguely uncomfortable with Vincent's presence beside me. My heart is racing, my vision is blurry, and all I can do is put one foot in front of the other.

We turn down Main Street and take a few steps in silence. Finally, I stop and turn toward him.

"What are you doing here, Vincent? Why are you here?"

He frowns and tries to reach toward me. I shrug him off and shake my head.

"Answer my question."

He takes a deep breath. "I wanted to see you, babe."

"Stop calling me that."

"You're mad, I get it," he says slowly. I can feel the anger bubbling up inside me as he tiptoes around my questions. All I want to know is the *truth*. I just want him to be straight with me, for once. I just want someone to tell me exactly what is going on.

"Vincent. You broke our engagement off after the hotel deal went south. Now, we're applying to be an official accommodation for the Park, and suddenly you're back?"

His eyebrows shoot up and his hand flies to his chest. I resist the urge to roll my eyes.

"Mara! Is that what you think of me?"

"It's what it feels like," I spit. "What am I supposed to think? *Why are you here*?"

"I'm here because I want you!" he exclaims. He puts a hand on my waist and my whole body tenses. "I made a mistake, letting you go. I got caught up with work and I didn't appreciate what was right in front of me. I should never have let you leave."

"*Let* me leave?" I repeat, raising my eyebrow. "You pretty much kicked me out, Vince."

"I did not," he says. "You know how it was between us. We

were falling apart." I make a noise to protest, shrugging his arm away, and he reaches over to take my hand in his. "That was mostly my fault, I'll admit that. I know it was. But I'm here now," he says.

I hate the way he's looking at me. I hate the way he can change his face from cold and heartless to charming in an instant. I hate the way that I'm not in control of my own emotions whenever he's around.

There's something different inside me now, though. I've found a new strength within me in the past few weeks. It feels like a shroud has been lifted from my eyes, and I can see everything just a little bit more clearly. I can see him for who he is, and his smooth words and charm-on-tap isn't having the same effect it had three years ago.

He takes a step toward me, still holding my hand. His face starts dipping toward mine and my heart starts hammering against my chest. Is he doing what I think he's doing...?

As he moves his head closer to mine, I put my hand on his chest and push him off.

"Vince! Get away from me!"

He takes a step back and a cloud passes over his face. The mask of charm falls away for an instant and I see the anger in his eyes. It's replaced in an instant with a placid look as he takes a step toward me.

"Don't be like this, babe. I need you!"

"Stop. Just stop," I say, shaking my head and backing away from him. "I don't want to talk to you. I don't want to see you!"

He catches my wrist in his and grabs me, pinching my skin. I yelp as he grips me tightly. I try to pull away but he keeps his hand on me, and that same flash of anger passes over his face. It disappears, and he lets go of my hand. I stumble backward and practically run back toward my parents' hotel.

By the time I make it to my room, I can't see straight. My heart is beating in my chest and I lock the doors before collapsing into bed. I rub my wrist where he's left red marks and feel the hot tears streaming down my face.

My chest feels hollow and pain pierces through my heart.

I've lost Dominic, and I can't trust my own family. I've never felt so alone.

29

DOMINIC

I TURN AWAY from the couple as they walk down Main Street. I've seen enough. I'd recognize Mara's fiancé anywhere, with his crisp clothing and his slicked-back hair. Seeing Mara with him is like a knife straight to the heart.

"Just take me home," I say to Ethan. He turns the car around and we drive in silence toward my house. When he stops the car, he looks at me without saying a word. I snort and chuckle bitterly.

"Like mother like daughter, hey?" I say, glancing at my brother. He looks away from me and grips the steering wheel a little bit harder.

"Maybe it wasn't what it looked like," he says.

I shake my head. "I don't know." *It looked like she was having a romantic stroll with her ex-fiancé.* Ethan nods to me and purses his lips. I nod back and open the door. I don't look back as I walk toward my little house. I hear him drive off, but all I do is walk into my tiny house and slam the door behind me.

Everything is a mess. I can't think. I walk straight to the refrigerator and crack open a beer. It's empty in a few seconds, and I crush the can in my hand and toss it in the trash. It falls into the bag with a soft thud, and I grab another one before slumping down onto the couch.

I turn the television on just to get some noise to drown out my thoughts.

Why was she with him?

What happened between her mother and my father?

What is happening between us?

Should I be doing this?

Every thought I have turns back toward the image of Mara and her ex on Main Street. They were a couple blocks away, but I couldn't mistake who he was. Not with that hair and those clothes. She didn't seem upset to be with him, not from where I was sitting.

The hot betrayal pierces through me and I guzzle some more beer. How could she? The very same day that her mother finds out I'm the one supplying the furniture, she runs back to her ex? Do I really mean so little to her?

I pace up and down my small house. The anger is bubbling up inside me and I try to hold it down. I try to control myself – to not get carried away. The anger just builds and builds and builds until I can't take it anymore.

I push my door open and stalk toward the workshop. There are half a dozen unfinished pieces for the hotel in there, and I look at them with disgust.

I'm a sellout.

I took her money and slept with her. For what?

I should have had more integrity. I'm no better than she is. I'm no better than her mother. What did my dad ever see in her anyway? For my entire life, I thought he was devoted to my mother – even after her death. But now it turns out he was *sleeping* with *Margaret McCoy* of all people?

I grab one of the nightstands that I finished this morning and carry it outside. I hurl it across the yard and it lands with a crunch. I walk to it and rip one of the legs off, throwing it off toward the trees. I stomp on the rest of the side table as it collapses under my weight. My lips curl into a snarl and I grunt as I smash the nightstand to kindling. I'm not thinking anymore, I'm just throwing and kicking and stomping until the sweat is dripping down my forehead.

I take a step back and look at the broken piece of furniture. It took me four days to make and ten minutes to destroy. My chest heaves up and down. My fists are clenching and unclenching as I stand there, looking at the destruction in my front yard.

There are bits of timber all over the grass. One of the legs of the table is near the edge of the trees, and the rest is unrecognizable. I sit on the grass and put my head in my hands, my chest still heaving up and down as I pant.

Before I know what's happening, tears are streaming down my face. I haven't cried in ten years – not since I was a teenager watching my father die before my eyes. I haven't cried since that day, but somehow today feels worse.

I thought I had something with Mara. I thought I meant something to her, in the way that she means to me. I thought I'd filled the hole in my heart and that I'd be able to find something more in these mountains.

I thought I could be happy.

I was an idiot. As my breathing turns to sobbing and the tears flow from my eyes, all I feel is betrayal. The tears burn my cheeks as they pour down my face, and I curl my hands into my hair, pulling it out as I rock back and forth.

Finally, I uncurl myself and stand up. My body feels stiff and sore as I make my way back toward my house. Before stepping through the doorway, I cast one last glance across my front yard. The stinging in my heart dulls as I look at the destruction I've wreaked on my own work.

I take a deep breath and turn my back on the broken furniture. I can't clean it up right now. I can't even look at it.

Everything reminds me of her. Everything reminds me of my dad, and the accident, and all the things that I never knew for all these years.

I don't know who my dad was, or who Margaret McCoy is, or why she still hates us. I don't know who Mara is, or if anything between us was even real.

All I know is that there's a hole in my heart and I can't think of anything except dulling the pain in my chest. I slam the door closed as I walk through it and forget about the carnage in the front yard. I go straight to the fridge and crack open another beer, ready to drown myself into oblivion.

I want to forget about it all. I want to turn back time and tell Mara to stay away from me. I want to forget what it feels like to have her body next to mine. Forget what she smells like. Forget her touch and her taste and her voice and her laugh. I want to forget everything.

I slump on the couch and drink until forgetting seems possible, and then I drink some more.

30

MARA

THERE'S a knock on the door and I jump. My father's voice comes through the door.

"Mara? Mara, are you okay?"

There's that question again – *Are you okay?* Why do people always seem to ask me that when I am most definitely *not* okay? I take a deep breath and sit up in bed.

"I'm fine, Dad. Just want to be on my own."

"Okay," he says through the door. It takes a few seconds before I hear his quiet footsteps pad back down the hallway. My throat closes and I blink back the tears that are gathering in my eyes.

I grab my phone and dial Dominic's number. The phone rings and rings until it goes to voicemail, and I hang up. I put my phone down for a few moments before trying him again.

Voicemail again.

I sigh, staring at the blank screen before sitting up. I turn to the back door of my room and take a deep breath before standing up.

I slip on my jacket and go outside. The sun is starting to go down and there's a cool breeze in the air. I let my feet take me toward Dominic's house. As I get closer, my heart starts beating harder and I wonder what I'm going to say to him. Last time I saw him, I saw pain and betrayal in his eyes before he got into Ethan's truck. Since then, I've been on a wild roller coaster ride. All I want is to have his arms around me and feel the comfort that I've had for the past few weeks.

I walk quickly through the forest as the last light of the afternoon filters through the trees. The path is carpeted in old pine needles, and I step over tree roots and rocks on my way to his house. The air smells fresh, and I take deep, cleansing breaths as I make my way toward his house.

With each step, I feel more comfortable. Everything will work out.

I know I don't want to be with Vincent. I saw the look in his eyes when his carefully crafted mask dropped, and I still have the marks on my wrist where he grabbed me. I saw the insistence with which my mother tried to push us together.

I'm not sure if she'll agree to finish the contract with Dominic. I'm not sure if Dominic wants to see me, or if he wants anything to do with me. All I know is that I have to talk to him. I have to tell him how I feel about him. I have to show him that he matters to me – that I'm not like my mother.

He *has* to understand that! He will, won't he?

With every step, my confidence grows. Soon, a smile is playing on my lips as I think of kissing him. I can almost feel his arms around me and the way that our bodies melt together. I can feel the happiness growing in my chest as I get closer to him.

When I round the last corner, that happiness starts to fade. I frown as the trees thin and his small log house comes into view. I sweep my eyes over his front yard and my heart drops.

There are splinters of wood everywhere. The remnants of a table or a nightstand are all over the grass. There's a leg near the edge of the tree-line, but the rest of the table is unrecognizable.

I take a few hesitant steps forward and my heart starts thumping.

Whatever it was, it's completely destroyed now. He must have smashed it over and over and over to get it to break this much. I pick up a piece of wood and turn it around in my hand, glancing toward the house. I look over at the workshop and see the door open.

I take a few slow steps as my heart hammers against my ribcage. With a deep breath, I peer inside the workshop and let out a sigh when I see it empty.

"Dominic?" I call out softly. I step inside and look around once more. "Dominic?"

I do a slow lap of the room, checking under the benches. I shake my head. Why would he be under there? When I'm sure the workshop is empty, I step back outside and close the door quietly behind me.

My breath is shallow as I tip-toe toward the house. The curtains are drawn, and I try to peek in the tiny opening between the edge of the window and the curtain. I can see a sliver of the room, but no sign of Dominic. My heart is racing now, and my palms are starting to sweat. I turn around and look at the destruction in the front yard one more time. What drove him to do this? Was it just seeing my mother upset at the hotel? Surely that wouldn't drive him this crazy.

I turn back toward the door and walk up to it. I ball up my fist and lift it up, taking one last deep breath as I try to slow down my racing heartbeat. I close my eyes and knock.

I hold my breath as I wait for his heavy footsteps.

Nothing.

I'm greeted with complete silence. I take another deep breath and knock again, a bit louder this time. "Dominic?" I call out. I wait again, counting the seconds of silence that follow.

Finally, I shake my shoulders and take a deep breath. I put my hand on the doorknob and turn it slowly, hoping to find it locked. If it's locked, I can turn around and go home. I can try to forget the smashed nightstand. I can call Dominic again later. I can figure out what's going on.

But it's not locked.

The doorknob turns in my hand, and I push the door open.

That's when I see him. He's collapsed on the sofa with crushed beer cans all around him. My hand flies up to my face in horror as I look at the state he's in. I take a step inside and hesitate, afraid to breathe.

Should I try to wake him? I glance behind me at the smashed table and my heart sinks.

Is this the man that I know? Is this the man that I've been falling for?

He would come home and destroy something in a fit of rage and then drink himself to sleep?

The happiness I felt on the walk over is completely gone. I don't know what to think, or how to feel, or what to do. I take a step toward him and accidentally kick a can. It spins on the floor toward him and knocks against his foot. My eyes widen and I wait for him to wake up, but he doesn't even stir. I watch him for a few moments as my chest squeezes.

I still care about him. I don't know what's going on, and I don't understand why he got upset and then drank himself to sleep, but I still want to be there for him.

Dominic's head is at an unnatural angle, so I grab a cushion from the couch and prop his head up. It's heavy, and he doesn't wake up as I move him. I grab a blanket from the end of the bed and cover him before laying a soft kiss on his temple. He stinks of beer and he starts snoring. I stroke my finger along his cheek, scratching his stubble and imagining him groaning in satisfaction.

My heart sinks as I walk back toward the door. I glance from the destruction in the front yard to the mess in the house, and I feel like crying. I take a deep breath and close the door before making the long, painful walk back toward the hotel.

My father's voice rings in my ears: *Are you okay?*

No, Dad. I'm definitely not okay. Not even close.

31

DOMINIC

My head is splitting. I try to sit up and groan as my whole body screams at me for moving. I squint at the pale light of dawn that filters through the window as I lift myself up. My blanket falls off and I look at the cushion behind me.

I don't remember getting those yesterday. I frown, looking around me at the crumpled cans of beer before dropping my head into my hands.

Ugh.

I shouldn't have done that. I've never been a drinker, and I've definitely never been one to drink myself into oblivion. I groan again as I brush the blanket off, looking at it one more time before leaning back on the sofa. I definitely don't remember getting that from the bedroom, but who knows. All I remember is drinking beer, after beer, after beer.

I hardly even flinch when there's a knock on the door. I sigh and bring my hands to my temples, rubbing them in slow circles to try to ease the pain radiating through my forehead. I don't care who's there. I just want to be left alone.

"Dominic!" Aiden's voice calls out. "Dominic!"

I sigh, groaning as I heave myself off the couch. What is

Aiden going to be mad about today? My feet drag on the floor as I make my way to the front door. I open it to see Aiden's concerned face.

"Dude, what the fuck happened here?" He asks, glancing at the yard. "What the fuck happened to you!"

I groan and turn around, collapsing back onto the couch as Aiden lets himself in. He closes the door behind him and looks around the room, shaking his head and blowing the air out of his nose.

"Dominic," he breathes.

"Don't, Aiden. Please," I say, closing my eyes and leaning back.

"This isn't you," he says. I open my eyes to see him sitting on the chair opposite me, studying my face as his eyebrows inch closer and closer together in consternation.

"I know," I reply. My head is still pounding, and I can barely string two words together.

"Here," Aiden says, walking to the kitchen and pouring a glass of water. "Drink this."

I nod in thanks and drain the glass. I empty it in seconds, and Aiden takes the glass from my hands and fills it up again. I drink half of it and finally take a deep breath.

"Thanks," I say. For the first time this morning, my voice comes out almost normal. Aiden sits down again and looks at me. I sigh and drop my forehead into my hands again.

"I don't know what happened," I say, looking at the floor. "I read that letter and then we came back and Mara was... I don't know what she was doing."

Aiden is silent for a few moments and I finally lift my head to look at him. He's staring out the window, chewing his lip as he thinks.

"You really care about her," he says after a pause.

His comment surprises me, and for a few moments I'm not

sure what to say. Finally, I take a deep breath and nod. "Yeah," I answer. "I do. I did, I mean..." I sigh. "Yeah."

He nods and swings his eyes back toward me. "I'm not mad at you for getting involved with her," he says.

My eyebrows shoot up. "No?" I ask.

Aiden chuckles. "Alright, maybe I was. But not anymore. I get it," he says. He smiles sadly and stares out the window again. "She always had this spark, even when we were kids."

"Look, if you don't want me to –"

"Nah," Aiden cuts me off, shaking his head. "I can't ask you to stop seeing her. I can't explain it," he says, leaning back in his chair. I take a drink of water and wait for him to continue. "I've looked at the McCoys as the enemy for so long. I blamed them for so much. Reading those letters this week..."

I snort. "Seems almost anticlimactic for it to all be because of a bad breakup between Dad and Margaret."

Aiden shakes his head and laughs softly. "I can't imagine the two of them together. But then again, I think about all the times she was over at our place. I thought it was to bring Mara over." Aiden looks at me, and his look pierces through me. "I thought the whole family was rotten to the core," he says. "But after reading those letters, I'm not so sure anymore."

"My head is all messed up," I admit. "I've got no idea what the fuck to think."

Aiden chuckles. "Same."

I take another drink of water and lean back on the sofa, resting my head back and closing my eyes. I can feel Aiden's gaze on me but I don't look at him. When he speaks, his voice is softer than I've ever heard it before.

"This isn't you, Dominic. That smashed up table outside, the drinking..."

I take a deep breath and look at my brother. I nod my chin

down once. "I know. I couldn't stand the thought of her with someone else."

"What are you going to do?"

Aiden is staring at me again, and I feel like my answer to this question is important. I wish I had something to tell him. I wish I could say what he wants me to say. I don't want to be fighting with my brothers. I don't want to be doubting Mara. I don't want to be drinking myself to sleep.

But as Aiden waits for me to answer, there's only one thing that comes to my mind. I take a deep breath and shake my head.

"I don't know," I say.

Aiden drops his eyes and nods his head up and down. He looks out the window again and takes a deep breath.

"I thought Dad's death was done ten years ago, but it seems to be getting more and more real every year."

"Who do you think knows about Dad and Margaret?" I ask.

Aiden looks at me and shrugs.

"You think Tim McCoy knows?" I say in a low voice.

My brother shrugs again and we exchange a loaded look.

"The more I think about it, the more Tim and Mara did nothing wrong," Aiden says. "All these years, I've blamed them all for Dad's death and for taking the business. But now..."

"It's all fucked up," I say. I stand up and stretch my body. Out of the corner of my eye, I see some shards of wood through the window. I take a few steps and look outside. I glance at Aiden, who has the hint of a smile playing on his lips.

"Thought you were in the business of making furniture, not destroying it," he says as the grin spreads across his face.

"Who the fuck knows anymore," I answer, turning back toward the kitchen and trying to hide my grin. "Like I said, it's all fucked up now."

32

MARA

I HAVEN'T SLEPT this badly since I left California. The last bad night's sleep I had was the night before moving back to Lang Creek. My whole body is aching as I lift myself up and get ready. I tiptoe to the kitchen and pour myself a strong cup of coffee before heading to the office.

The renovations are well underway, and even if Dominic stays on board with the job, we have a mountain of work to do in order to finish on time. I can't think of Dominic right now, or Vincent, or anything. I just want to bury myself in work and feel something other than sadness.

I fire up my computer and start working. Soon, my bad night's sleep is forgotten and I'm completely absorbed in my work.

I'm so focused that I don't hear the door open behind me. It's not until Vincent's voice rings in my ears that my spine straightens and I spin around in my chair. He's standing in the doorway with my mother, wearing a smug grin on his face as he watches me.

"Hard at work?" he asks. His eyebrow is raised in that arrogant smirk that I've always despised. I look from him to my mother and back at him.

"You're still here?" I respond. "I don't want to see you."

"Mara," my mother says, sashaying through the doorway toward me. "Don't be like that."

"I'm an adult, Mother. I'll speak however I want to speak."

Her eyebrows shoot up and she stops in her tracks. She looks taken aback by my words but recovers quickly.

"I raised you to be polite," she chides.

"You raised me to be a doormat," I spit. "Well, not anymore."

"Mara!"

"Mrs. McCoy," Vincent interjects. "Please, allow me." He takes a step in and closes the door. The room immediately feels stuffy. Vincent's body is blocking the doorway, and my mother is looming just beside me. I try to keep my face still but my heart is hammering against my ribcage. I'm scared.

Vincent grabs a chair and turns it toward me. He sits down and crosses one ankle over his knee as he tents his fingers under his chin. He stares at me with those beady eyes, with one side of his mouth curled up in a smirk. *How I was ever attracted to him??*

"Mara," he says. I suppress a shiver. Even the way he says my name disgusts me now. "I've been speaking to your mother over the past few weeks."

My eyebrows shoot up and I glance at my mother. *Weeks?* She ignores me.

"We've come to an understanding."

"About what?" I snap. Vincent leans back in his chair and almost snarls at me. My mother flutters around and finally leans against the wall beside the door.

"About our engagement," Vincent finally replies.

I snort. "What engagement? That was called off a couple months ago, or have you forgotten about that?"

"Mara, please," my mother says. I swing my eyes toward her and feel the anger bubbling up inside me. Is this real life? Are they really in here, telling me to reconsider my engagement with this man?

"Mara," Vincent says. His voice is dark and his eyes are unreadable. A chill goes down my spine and I find myself waiting for him to speak again. "If you want your little boyfriend to have any chance of being successful, you'll be reasonable."

My blood runs cold and I stare at him, not understanding. "What are you talking about?"

"Your mother and I have agreed to renew our business relationship. But in order to get your father to agree, we need to be a happy couple."

"*My mother and you agreed?*" I start, staring at him with my mouth wide open. "Am I not a person to you?" I ask, turning to my mother. "Do I not get a say in this?"

My blood is pumping and the outrage is boiling inside me. All the resentment and betrayal I felt when my engagement fell apart is coming back to me. Vincent leans back in his chair and smirks.

"If you don't agree, I'll use every connection I have to make sure that your lover's little woodworking business gets run into the ground."

I stare at him, opening and closing my mouth as I struggle to find words. Is he threatening me? Why is he doing this?

"What are you getting out of this?"

"Well, with this hotel approved by the Park, we'll be able to expand the brand nationwide. We don't need another luxury hotel here, but we can have McCoy hotels in every National Park in the country."

My heart sinks and tears start prickling my eyes.

"And if I refuse?"

"If you refuse," Vincent replies slowly, "then your career as a designer will be over. The Clarkes will see everything they touch turn to dust."

"You don't have that kind of power," I spit, eyes blazing as I stare at the man I used to love.

He grins and I see nothing but evil in his face. "Try me," he says.

My chest is hollow. I look from him to my mother. She's staring at me, and I see nothing in her eyes. She's completely devoid of emotion, and for the first time I see her for who she truly is.

The loving, friendly woman that she portrays is all an act. She's nothing but a vindictive, greedy leech on this town. I blink back tears and try to swallow as my throat tightens.

I think of Dominic, and the effort that he puts into every piece of furniture he makes. I think of his workshop, impeccably clean. I think of the way that he runs his fingers over a piece of wood with something almost like reverence.

He could lose it all. His brothers could lose it all. I try to blink back tears but I can't. They're pouring down my cheeks as I think of the man I love losing everything he cares about.

I can't do that to him. I can't be the reason that once again, the Clarke brothers lose everything.

I lift my eyes to Vincent and I swallow the disgust that rises in my throat. Without a word, I nod my head down once.

With that, my fate is sealed. I've traded my future for Dominic's. The tears are pouring down my cheeks and my chest feels like it's been smashed with a sledgehammer.

As much as it hurts, I know it's the right decision.

I'm the reason he lost his father. I'm the reason he lost his father's business. I can't be the reason he loses his livelihood. I brush the hot tears away from my cheeks and try to sit up straighter.

Vincent puts his hands on his knees and stands up. He looks down at me with that arrogant smirk on his lips.

"Good decision," he says. "You'd better pack now. We leave tomorrow."

"What!" I say, snapping my head up toward him. My mother clears her throat.

"You and Vincent will go back to Silicon Valley. I'll manage the rest of the renovations. Vincent and I have agreed to keep Dominic's contract in place, as a show of good faith to you."

My jaw is on the floor, and all I can do is look from one of them to the other. *A show of good faith?* Is she fucking kidding? She thinks she's doing me a *favor*?

Based on the state of Dominic's front yard, I'm not even sure he'll want to keep working for my mother. I open my mouth to speak, but she and Vincent are already out the door. They leave the door open and all I can do is stare after them.

My head is reeling. I feel like I'm falling through space, and I don't know which direction is up and which is down.

Pack your bags, Vincent said to me.

I finally turn to the window and look at the mountains that I grew up with. A tear falls down my cheek and I put my head in my hands.

I've lost everything now. Maybe it's karma, for causing Mr. Clarke to lose his life. Maybe letting the Clarke brothers live in peace is my atonement, and I deserve all of this.

I was kidding myself when I thought I could make it up to them with this business deal. The best way to make it up to them is to leave forever and never come back.

33

DOMINIC

IT TAKES me half an hour to clean up the destruction in the front yard. I look at the pile of broken timber and sigh, throwing it all into my box of kindling. At least I can make use of the table, even if it is just to burn it.

Burning things to ash seems to be my specialty.

I cast my eye over the front yard and take a deep breath. It's clean now, and Mara won't have to see it like that. My cheeks burn as I think of her.

I've been acting like a child having a temper tantrum. It's not like me. I let my emotions get the better of me when what I should be doing is talking to her.

I'm not sure if I still have a job, but all I know how to do is work, so I walk toward the workshop. I throw open the big garage door and let the sunlight fill the space. I look at the mountain of half-finished work and put my hands on my hips. I've got a lot to do.

I get to work, and pretty soon the cobwebs in my mind have cleared away. With every cut of my saw, every mark of my pencil, and every measurement of my tape, my head is a little bit clearer.

Within two hours, I have the frame for a new nightstand built and assembled.

Taking a step back, I look at my work and sigh. This is what I should be doing, not drinking and smashing things. I should be working and building things up. I walk over to my mini-fridge and take out a bottle of water, emptying it in one gulp. As I finish it, I hear a car pulling up the drive. I lean against the wall and wait to see who rounds the bend.

When I see Margaret McCoy's car, I start to frown.

Is she here to tell me I'm fired? Why isn't Mara with her?

Margaret stops the car outside and gets out. She's wearing a Jackie-O type suit with perfectly styled hair. Her oversized sunglasses cover most of her face and she smiles at me with her bright red lips. I try not to shiver. I take a few steps toward her and wait for her to speak.

"Dominic!" She calls out. I grunt. She takes a deep breath and paints a smile on her face. "I wanted to apologize," she continues.

For what? For cheating on your husband with my father? For stealing his business?

"Okay," I grunt.

"I've been an absolute ninny. Your work for the hotel has been exquisite. I hope my reaction hasn't put you off. I've been thinking that maybe this is the perfect way to put all this silliness behind us."

Silliness?

I grunt again and she smiles a bit wider. It seems to be a struggle for her to smile hard enough, but I just nod.

"So you still want the furniture?"

"Of course!" She says with that smile still plastered over her face. "You do such wonderful work. Don't you think it's great that our families are able to work together again?"

"Yeah," I reply, not knowing what else to say. She looks at me for a few moments and I see the edges of her smile start to droop. She nods her head and claps her hands together.

"Well, that's settled! I'll be taking over from Mara when she leaves. If you could send me a schedule of completion, that would be great."

Alarm bells start to go off in my head. "Mara's leaving? Where is she going?"

"Oh!" Margaret titters. "Of course! You didn't know!" She laughs again and waves her hands. My heart starts thumping and I just want to tell her to spit it out already. She smiles again and tilts her head to the side. "Mara's fiancé Vincent came back! They're off to Silicon Valley in the morning. Isn't that *wonderful!*"

I hardly hear what she says. Her voice sounds like it's coming at me from under water and my vision starts to tunnel.

I knew it.

I know what I saw. I knew it was him. I've been such an idiot! To think that Mara would be with me. To think that she wouldn't run back to the rich billionaire she'd been engaged to at the first opportunity.

Margaret McCoy says something but I don't hear it. I turn back toward the workshop and vaguely hear her car start. I close the doors and slump down on a chair as I try to process what I've just learned.

She's leaving.

She's leaving *tomorrow.*

She's leaving tomorrow *with her fiancé!*

How could I be so fucking stupid! I can't believe I thought I meant something to her. The anger from yesterday starts welling up inside me and I try to push it down. My head is spinning. The clarity that I had just a few minutes ago is replaced with a tornado of thoughts.

She's *leaving.*

I can hardly believe it. I finally lift my head and look around the room, trying to understand what's going on. Did the past few weeks mean nothing? Why is her mother all of a sudden so nice to me? Why does she still want me to work for her?

Why did her fiancé come back?

The urge to destroy something bubbles up inside me but I shake my head. I'm not going to turn into that person. I'm not going to let myself get carried away like that again. I'm not going to drink my troubles away and I'm not going to destroy anything else.

The workshop feels stuffy. My vision blurs and nausea comes over me like a tidal wave. I throw open the door and rush outside, leaning against the wall as my stomach churns.

Bile and acid and alcohol come out of my stomach as I retch against the workshop. I vomit over and over into the grass until my body calms down and I'm able to stand up. My mouth tastes vile and my eyes are watering, but all I can do is lean against the workshop and breathe in and out.

My head is a mess. Mara is leaving. I'm still working for the McCoys. I open my eyes and stare at the blue sky. I let the sunshine warm up my skin and I take a few deep breaths.

When I'm able to breathe normally again, my shoulders relax and one clear thought comes to me.

Something isn't adding up.

There's something about this whole thing that just doesn't make sense. Something is wrong, but I can't figure it out. It's too rushed, too unexpected. Mara couldn't have been lying to me this whole time, could she?

I shake my head.

Something isn't right.

34

MARA

THE HORROR from yesterday has been replaced with numbness. I zip up my suitcase and stand it up, walking to my bedroom door and opening it.

At least I didn't have to share his bed.

My father is walking toward the back of the house with a concerned expression on his face. He helps me with my suitcase and turns toward me, searching my face.

"Are you sure this is what you want, Mara? It's all so quick! What's going on?"

A pang goes through my chest when I look into my father's eyes. I don't want to lie to him. I don't want to lie to Dominic. I don't want to leave, but what can I do? The only way for me to protect Dominic is to do what Vincent and my mother want me to do.

I swallow and force a smile onto my face.

"I'm sure, Dad." I open my mouth to say something else, but I can't think of anything. My father puts his hand on my shoulder and stares into my eyes until I have to look away.

"Mara," he says softly. "What's going on?"

I force myself to look at him again as I straighten my shoulders. "I'm getting married, Dad. That's what's going on."

"Why does it sound like a funeral, then? Mara, does this have anything to do with what you were saying before? About using you? Is there something I don't know?"

I shake my head. "Dad, please. I'm just tired. I was up late packing all my things. This is what I want to do. I want to go with Vincent."

I hope that my voice is convincing. I hope he believes me, and he stops looking at me like that. I hope that I can just leave this town behind me and that the pain in my chest will fade.

My father sighs and nods his head. "You know you can talk to me, right? If something is wrong? I know your mother is bullheaded sometimes, but that doesn't mean you have to change your life for her."

I grimace as I try to smile at my father. "I'm not changing my life for her," I say. *I'm doing it for him.*

My father nods and takes a deep breath. "Better get going then," he says.

It's a somber walk from my little room at the back of the hotel to the front lobby. Vincent is there, with his sunglasses on and his hair slicked back. My mother is waiting near the door, and I pass both of them without saying anything. I walk straight out the door to the waiting car. My father follows with my suitcases, and I help him load all my things up into the trunk.

As I'm putting the last of my bags in the car, a truck rumbles down the road. I can almost sense Dominic's eyes on me, even before I look up to see his vehicle. Our eyes meet as he pulls up in front of the hotel. My mother flutters down the pathway toward him, calling out for help behind her.

"Dominic! I wasn't expecting you until tomorrow! Do you have a delivery already?"

"Finished early," he says, not looking at her. Our eyes are

locked on each other. He's asking me a thousand wordless questions and I can't do anything except stand there. My heartbeat sounds like a hurricane in my ears, and it feels like the earth has shifted on its axis. I'm off-balance, and all I can do to stay standing is stare at the man I love.

Every part of my body is screaming to run to him. I want to wrap my arms around him and kiss him and never let him go. A light breeze ruffles his hair. He stands next to his truck and looks at me as if nothing else in the world exists. If I took three steps, I could be in his arms. I could wrap myself around him and tell Vincent to leave me alone.

But what then?

Dominic's career would be ruined. Vincent might go after Ethan and Aiden as well. I'd be the cause of all their pain once again, just as I was ten years ago.

Vincent appears beside me and puts his hand on the small of my back. A shiver of disgust passes through me and I try to step away from him. I shift my gaze to the ground. He urges me toward the car and I let myself be led to the passenger's side door. It slams closed and I see Dominic in the mirror, standing exactly as he was. He's staring at the car, and then shifts his gaze to Vincent.

I wish I could hear what Vincent says to him, but I can't. In a few moments, he's sliding into the driver's side and the car is rumbling to life.

My parents raise their arms in goodbye and I see my father's eyebrows knit together. He knows something is wrong, but he won't say it. I blink back the tears that are gathering in my eyes and shift my gaze forward.

This is my life now.

Vincent turns on the radio and I lean my head against the window. I close my eyes and try to forget the look on Dominic's face when I got in the car.

When we pass the sign on the edge of town that says, 'Thank

you for visiting Lang Creek!', my heart breaks all over again. The sharp pain radiates from my chest to every part of my body until I have to close my eyes and focus on my breathing just to stop myself from screaming.

Vincent reaches over and puts his hand on my thigh. I tense, snapping my head toward him and snarling:

"Don't touch me."

He raises an eyebrow and takes his hand away, placing it back on the steering wheel. He glances over at me and shakes his head.

"You're going to have to play the loving wife eventually, Mara. This kind of thing won't fly."

"You're the Devil," I say as my voice catches in my throat.

"I haven't done this alone, remember. Your own family sold you out."

He doesn't look at me when he says it, but I know he's watching my every reaction. A lump forms in my throat and I try to blink back the tears that are gathering in my eyes.

As much as I hate him – as much as I hate to admit it – he's right. It wasn't just him. It was my mother too. She's the reason I'm here. She's the reason the Clarkes hate us. She's the reason that I've just left the love of my life behind to fend for himself.

The further we drive from Lang Creek, the more the horror of my situation starts to set in. I'm going back to Silicon Valley. I'm going back to the land of fake people and fake smiles. I'm going back to the land of money. Vincent's world. I glance out the windows at the mountains around us and say a silent farewell.

35

DOMINIC

I KNOW MARA. I've known her my whole life, and I've gotten to know her very well over the past few weeks. At least, I think I know her.

I know that I've never seen her look like that. When that arrogant asshole Vincent touched her, she almost recoiled in disgust. The look on her face was pure despair. I watch them drive away and feel something inside me die.

She's gone.

Just like that. No warning, no goodbye, no word from her at all.

I shift my gaze to her parents, and for a moment I meet Mr. McCoy's gaze. His eyebrows are drawn together, and the tip of his nose is bright red. He's grinding his teeth together as he looks at me, and then he looks back toward the road where Mara disappeared.

I watch him tuck his chin into his chest and stomp back into the hotel. Margaret McCoy appears by my side and starts inspecting the furniture I'm delivering. She's got that fake smile plastered over her face and she says things I don't hear.

I couldn't sleep last night, and I stayed up all night finishing the pieces. She nods approvingly and clicks her fingers toward the two waiting hotel workers. My lip lifts in disgust as they jump forward and start unloading the furniture. She doesn't even treat them like people.

I grab a corner and help them load the furniture up into one of the newly renovated rooms. I look around the room at the fresh paint, the hardwood floors and the simple rug that Mara chose. I see her in every detail of the decor – from the wall sconces that she chose to the way the furniture fits perfectly with the style of the hotel.

She's talented.

She's *gone*.

I clear my throat to try to stop myself from tearing up. I help place the new furniture and leave the two hotel workers to their work, going back down to my truck. On the way out, I catch a glance of Tim McCoy in Mara's office. He's standing there, looking at her empty desk as if she's going to appear in front of him. I glance over my shoulder and when I see he's alone, I walk over toward him.

He turns around when I clear my throat.

"Dominic," he says, turning toward me. He extends his hand to shake mine. "I'm so impressed with your work. You're a true talent."

"Thank you," I respond. He clears his throat and avoids my gaze. We stand in front of each other, waiting for the other to speak. Finally, I take a deep breath.

"Mara..." My voice trails off and Tim shakes his head.

"Something's not right," he interrupts. He glances at the door and moves to close it. When we're alone in the office, he looks out the window and then back to me. "Something's not right about this whole thing. Mara didn't want that."

My heart starts thumping as he looks at me. *I knew it.* I'm simultaneously elated that she didn't want to go with Vincent, and horrified that she did.

"What the fuck is going on, then?"

Tim McCoy stares at me for a few long moments. His eyes narrow and he looks into my eyes until I have to force myself to maintain eye contact with him. He finally nods.

"It was you, wasn't it?"

"It was me what?" I ask. My heart starts beating a bit harder.

"I thought Mara was seeing someone. She was so happy." He chuckles and shakes his head. "I should have known. Why else would she keep you a secret? She's always told me everything."

"I…" I look at Tim and finally take a deep breath. "I care about her."

"I can tell. I could tell by the way you looked at her when she was getting in the car. I'm telling you, Dominic, something isn't right."

I look at the man that has been on the other side of this stupid feud for ten years, and I remember the letters on Aiden's kitchen table. How would he react if he knew that his wife had been cheating on him all those years ago? Did he know?

When I think of Margaret McCoy's face when she watched Mara leave, all I feel is disgust. Disgust for her, and disgust for my father for ever having been involved with her. Was she always this *evil*? What did my father ever see in her?

Tim McCoy is staring at me and I take a deep breath.

"What do you think is going on?"

"I'm not sure, but I'd say my wife has something to do with it. Mara said something to me a few weeks ago. Something funny. She said that we'd sold her off as a bargaining chip in a business deal for the new hotel. I told her she was wrong, but now…"

"You think it was Margaret?"

Tim's face scrunches together and he shakes his head. "I don't think she'd be capable of something like that. She's always been a good woman. A good wife. A good mother. Why...?"

A pang goes through my chest and the words are on the tip of my tongue. I want to tell him about his wife. I want to tell him about what she did, and why she took our business, but I don't know how. Tim sighs and shakes his head.

"I'll get to the bottom of this." He looks up at me and puts a hand on my shoulder. "Dominic, don't tell anyone about this conversation. Can you do that?"

I nod my chin down once. "I won't. If there's anything you need... I mean, if Mara is in trouble..."

Tim's lips curl up into a sad smile. "I wish it was you she was running away with. I've wanted to bury the hatchet between our two families ever since that business with the trucking company happened. I want you to know –"

"Tim, stop," I interrupt. "It's okay. There are no hard feelings. Not anymore. Mara..." I take a deep breath. "Mara showed me what kind of person she is. If you have one tenth of the heart that she does, then there's no need for us to be fighting."

I see Tim swallow and nod his head. His eyes look bright when he looks away. He clears his throat and takes a deep breath before grabbing the office door handle and opening the door.

"Right. Well. Let's get this thing figured out."

We nod at each other and I walk out of the hotel. It's not until I'm in my truck and driving back toward my house that I let out a huge sigh.

I knew something was wrong. I don't know what it is yet, or how to fix it, but I do know one thing: Mara didn't want to leave with Vincent.

That thought carries me all the way home. She didn't want to leave with Vincent. She wanted to stay with me. Whatever it was that was pushing her to leave, I'm going to figure it out.

Something inside me wakes up. It's the familiar anger that carried me through the past ten years. It's the anger that led me to light the new hotel on fire and burn it to the ground. It's the anger that Mara started to mend. I don't want to be an angry person, but right now I can use that anger for good. I can get Mara back.

36

———

MARA

Everything reminds me of Dominic. As we drive through the forest, I remember how he used to hold my hand as we walked through the trees. I remember the way he always smelled like fresh pine and sawdust after a day of work. When we board the plane, I think about how big he would have looked in the tiny airplane seats. When Vincent grabs my hand with his cold, clammy fingers, I think of the way Dominic was always warm and gentle with me.

When I look at Vincent, all I feel is disgust. He doesn't see me as a person. He sees me as a ticket to expanding his empire. What happens when he doesn't need me anymore, I wonder? What happens when the contracts are signed and the new hotels are built? What happens when he's made all the money he can make from our union?

He'll toss me aside like a piece of trash and move on to his next victim. I know he will. Did my mother think of that? Did she think of anything except herself and her bank account?

We drive up to the luxurious estate that I used to call home. The tall, wrought-iron gates open and our black sedan glides through. The estate feels more like a prison than a home. We make our way up the winding drive toward the big driveway loop in front of the house and I see the huge gaudy fountain in the center of the circle. I take a deep breath and try to contain my disgust. Everything about this house – everything I used to love and be in awe of – it's so ugly now.

I miss Lang Creek. I miss the fresh air and the wind in my hair. I miss the calming presence of the mountains around me and the smell of pine trees and fresh air.

I miss *Dominic.*

Every time I think of him, a hot dagger passes through my heart. The black sedan stops in front of the steps and I open the door, stretching my body as I stand up and look at my new prison. Vincent circles around the car and hops up the steps.

"Will is coming out to help you with your bags. I'll be in my office. Don't bother me with anything," he says without looking at me. He disappears through the tall wood-paneled front door and suddenly I'm alone again. I turn away from the house and can see glimpses of the tall black fence that surrounds the property.

How did this place never feel like a prison before?

"Hi, Miss McCoy," the concierge calls out. I turn to see him and smile at the familiar face. "I wasn't expecting to see you back here."

I chuckle. "I wasn't expecting to be back, Will. Thanks," I say as he starts unloading my bags. "How are the kids?"

"They're great! Melissa just started kindergarten and I can't believe it. They're growing up so fast."

A pang passes through my heart when I see his eyes shining. I know that's something I'll never have now. His happiness when he talks about his wife and kids is so obvious. I hate how jealous I am.

The rest of the day is a blur. The house, the staff, the neighbors – they're all familiar, but somehow, I feel like a stranger. I feel like I've changed. Maybe I can finally see it for what it is: empty and fake.

I eat dinner alone and then watch TV alone. I go on my phone and scroll through social media and then boredom starts to creep in.

As I toss my phone aside with a sigh, it dings. I look at the screen and my heart starts thumping. Dominic's name flashes across it. I look around the room to make sure I'm alone.

"You okay?"

There's that question again.

I stare at the two words on the screen for a minute before taking a deep breath. Somehow it seems more real when it's coming from Dominic.

You okay?

I read it and re-read it over and over and over. What am I supposed to answer? *No, I'm not okay. I'm far from okay. I miss you. I love you.*

Or maybe I can lie. *I'm fine.*

I could tell him not to contact me. I could ignore him.

My fingers hover over my phone as I read those two little words over and over. I hear a door open and close down the hall and my head snaps around. I'm still alone. I look back at my phone and feel my heart drop.

I know what I have to do. I can't talk to him or maintain any kind of relationship with him. My heart breaks all over again when I start typing a response. My fingers are trembling and my eyes blur as the tears start to fill them.

. . .

166

"*Please don't contact me again. Good luck with the furniture, I wish you the best.*"

My fingers are shaking so much I can't press send right away. I put my phone down and let the tears flow down my cheeks. I jump when my phone buzzes again. It's a picture from Dominic.

"*Made you this:*"

I start laughing through my tears when I see the little cup full of pens, carved out of a piece of wood. I think of that day in my room, when he knocked over all my pens and pencils. It was the first time I saw that glimmer of humor in his eye. It was the first time I saw the real him. I stare at the picture and a warmth passes through my heart. It starts beating again and it feels like I'm alive for the first time since Vincent appeared in Lang Creek.

I erase my message and type a new one.

"*I love it.*"

I press send and hold my phone to my chest. I close my eyes and let the tears flow down my cheeks. I know I shouldn't talk to him. I should delete his number. But when I look back at the photo of the wooden cup full of pens, I feel more love from Dominic than I've ever felt from Vincent.

Dominic sends me another message.

. . .

"Post office is closed. You'll have to come get it yourself."

My chest squeezes and my hands start trembling all over again.
I glance over my shoulder one more time and type out a quick
response.

"I wish I could."

I exit out of the text and delete it in a couple taps. I scroll
through my phone and find Dominic's number, deleting it from
my contacts. My heart is thumping and I know I shouldn't be
talking to him. I shouldn't be encouraging him.

But my God, it feels good.

37

DOMINIC

"I wish I could."

I read the words over and over as I lie back in bed. That means that she's there against her will. It means they're holding something over her. It means her father is right.

I jump out of bed and pull on my pants and jacket. I don't bother tying my shoes – I just pull them on and rush out the door. My truck rumbles to life, and I peel out of the driveway and turn off toward the mountains. I drive faster than I should down the highway toward my brother's house. When I make it to the big house, nestled on the side of the mountain, the porch light comes on and Aiden opens the door to greet me.

"Dominic! What are you doing here so late?"

"I need your help."

My brother stares at me as I walk toward him. His eyes search my face and I can imagine what he sees. I'm sure my clothes are disheveled and my hair is all over the place. I can imagine the look in my eyes. He looks at me for a few moments and nods his head.

"Come in." We walk to the kitchen in silence. "Coffee?"

"Sure," I answer.

I slump down onto a chair as he makes a pot of coffee. He places a mug in front of me, and then takes one for himself before sitting down across from me.

"What's going on?"

I take a deep breath.

"Mara's gone."

Aiden frowns. "Gone?"

I nod. "Gone. She left with her ex this morning."

"Fuck..."

I shake my head. "No, it's not like that. Something's wrong. Look," I pull out my phone and show him the messages. He reads through them and frowns.

"Dominic," he starts. "I don't want you to get your hopes up. This isn't..."

"No," I interrupt. "You should have *seen* her when she was leaving. It was like someone died. Tim McCoy pulled me aside and said he thought something was going on. And now she's saying she wishes she could leave? Something is wrong. Something is really wrong."

Aiden takes a deep breath and reads the messages again. He takes a sip of coffee and places the mug back down. Finally, he lifts his eyes to mine and shrugs.

"What do you want to do? What can you do? What can *I* do?"

"Give me the letters," I say.

Aiden's eyes widen and he shakes his head. "No."

"Aiden! It's the only way. I'll bring them to Tim. He'll see his wife for who she is and then we can confront her. We can figure this thing out!"

"You want us to drag Dad's memory through the dirt? You want the whole town to know he was having an affair with a married woman? I can't do that to him!"

"He did it, Aiden! He did it to himself!"

Aiden stares at me and shakes his head. "I can't do it. It would start this feud all over again."

"Aiden," I start. I can feel my throat closing and my eyes watering. I'm begging my brother with my eyes as I put my palms flat on the table. I swallow and take a deep breath. "Aiden, I love her," I finally say.

Aiden says nothing, he just looks at me.

"I love her, and she's been taken away from me. Dad... Dad would understand."

Aiden's face scrunches and he looks at the floor. I can see the turmoil inside him as he shakes his head. He looks up at me and the depth of his pain is visible in his eyes. His voice comes out as a whisper.

"I can't, Dominic. I can't put his dirty laundry on display like that. What would people think of him? What would people think of *us*?"

"Give him the letters," says a voice behind me. The two of us jump and turn to see Aiden's wife, Madeline, in the doorway. She's holding her robe closed and has sleep in her eyes. She's staring at Aiden and they exchange a wordless glance.

"Give him the letters, Aiden," she says again, more softly this time. "Your father has been gone for ten years, and you have a chance to do something good. You have a chance to fix this silly feud once and for all. Isn't that worth it? Isn't that what he would have wanted?"

Aiden's eyebrows are drawn together and it looks like he's about to start sobbing. He's wringing his hands and taking deep breaths. Madeline takes a few steps toward him and puts her hands on his shoulders. When she touches him, he crumples. A huge sob rakes through his body and Maddy wraps her arms around him, whispering in his ear. He lifts his hand to hers and takes deep breaths as she calms him down.

I watch them and my heart breaks.

I want that.

I want a woman who knows me inside and out. I want a woman who can point me in the right direction and help me make difficult decisions.

I want Mara.

Aiden finally lifts his eyes to mine and dips his chin down.

"Okay," he relents. "I'll give you the letters."

My chest squeezes and I nod to my brother. "Thank you," I answer.

When he hands me the stack of letters, he puts his hand on my shoulder and looks me straight in the eye. "I hope this works," he says.

I snort and shake my head. "So do I, Aiden. So do I."

He nods his head and steps aside as Maddy wraps her arms around me.

"Thank you," I whisper in her ear as she gives me a hug. She pulls away and smiles at me.

"Get her back, Dominic. She's worth it."

My throat tightens and I look at the stack of papers in my hand. This is the key. I know it is. This will convince Tim to look at his wife differently. This will convince him that Mara is in real trouble, and she's doing something against her will.

I don't know why. I don't know what they're holding over her, but I'll die before I let her be taken away from me.

38

MARA

THE GUEST BEDROOM in Vincent's house is bigger than our biggest suite at the hotel back home. I wake up in the plush, comfortable bed and all I can think is that I'd rather be in Dominic's tiny cabin. I roll over and look out the window, seeing the bright California sunshine already streaming through the windows.

With a groan, I sit up and rub the sleep from my eyes. My stomach growls and I take a deep breath, getting up and tiptoeing down the stairs toward the kitchen. Vincent's office door is ajar, and as I'm walking up to it, I overhear a snippet of his conversation.

"... no, no, that's fine. Just take him off the list of approved suppliers for the other hotels. We'll let him finish out this contract. Yep, with an 'e'. C-L-A-R-K-E. Thanks."

My blood runs cold and I strain my ears to hear more, taking another step closer to the door. I jump when it swings open.

"Oh! Vincent! Hi! Good morning!" I stutter, taking a step backward and trying to regain my composure. He's already dressed in a full suit with his hair slicked back, and he looks me up and down before glancing at his watch. My cheeks start to burn as I think of my nightgown and unwashed hair. I'm not used to being dressed to the nines all the time.

"There's coffee in the kitchen," he says before glancing at me. "You got any plans today?"

I stifle a scoff, and then try to shrug casually. "Might go see the girls," I answer vaguely. He nods and closes his office door before heading off toward the front of the house.

"I'll see you tonight. Don't wait for me for dinner." He walks away without looking back and I try to ignore the sting in my chest. I hear the front door open and close, and I duck into the front room to see him driving away. Once he's out of view, I walk back toward the office and glance up and down the hallway. I put my hand on the doorknob as my heart starts thumping against my ribcage. My mouth has gone dry and I close my eyes for an instant before turning the knob.

Locked.

"Shit," I say under my breath.

"Looking for something?" I jump at the sound of Will's voice and turn to see him in the hallway. My hand flies to my chest and I laugh nervously.

"Will! You scared me," I say as the flush creeps into my cheeks. I pat my hair and tuck it behind my ears before glancing at the door again. "I was just, uh... Vincent asked me to sign some papers for the engagement. He said they were in his office, so I assumed it would be unlocked."

I'm so bad at lying, I'm sure Will is going to call me out right away. Instead, he nods his head and pulls out a set of keys.

"The boss has started locking it lately, I'm not sure why. I think he's forgotten I still have the key," he says, sliding the key into the lock and turning it smoothly. "Just let me know when you're done. I'll lock it back up."

I nod and slip into the office, closing the door behind me. I take a moment to lean against the door with my eyes closed, taking a deep breath to calm my nerves.

That was close.

What happens if Will tells Vincent? What will I say? I shake my head and focus on the huge oak desk that looms in front of me. I'll cross that bridge when I come to it.

I walk behind the desk and flip open the laptop. It's password protected, obviously. I hover my hands over the keyboard and sigh. I'd have no idea what his password is. Instead, I flip open a manila folder that's laying to the side of the computer. I frown when I see the papers inside.

"This is my application," I whisper to myself. I flip through the pages and see my application to the Parks, and the signed page that recognizes my parent's hotel as official accommodation. I frown, staring at the approval. I didn't know this had come through!

I look at the date and my eyebrows shoot up. It's dated a week before Vincent appeared in Lang Creek. *He moves fast.*

I flip through the papers and see a duplicate of my application. My heart starts thumping when I look at the proposal. Vincent wants to build half a dozen more hotels, and he wants to use my family's name. I turn the pages over until one page catches my eye. It's got a red pen mark through one line.

The top of it reads "Approved Suppliers List", and the name that's crossed off is near the bottom of the list: Dominic Clarke, Furniture Maker.

"You motherfucker," I breathe. The anger starts coiling inside me and my heart starts to beat faster. My hands are trembling as I close the folder back up and shut the laptop screen down. I slip out of the room to see Will waiting outside.

"Found what you were looking for?" He asks cheerily.

I force a smile. "Yep!" I head off toward the kitchen as my head fills with questions.

Even though I'm here, and I've done everything they asked – even giving up my relationship with Dominic – they're *still* going to fuck him over! They're still going to remove his name from the approved supplier list which means he won't have an uptick in business. The whole reason he agreed to do this was to grow his business, and now that reason is gone.

They lied to me. Vincent, my mother – they both lied through their teeth. They told me his business would be safe, and now they're doing everything they can to cut it down.

I'm furious now. My cheeks are burning and my hands are shaking so hard I can't even pour myself a cup of coffee. I take a deep breath and try again, but all I can think of is Dominic.

I can deal with betrayal when I'm the victim. As painful as it is, I can deal with my mother using me. I can deal with having a loveless marriage to a man I despise, if it means that Dominic gets to live a good life. But now? He doesn't even get that. He gets nothing.

It's not even anger anymore – it's fury. I've never felt like this before. My whole body feels like it's vibrating and all I can see is Vincent's snarling face. I forget about the coffee and stalk back down the hallway.

"Will!" I call out. "Will!"

His head appears around the corner.

"Give me your keys," I say before he can speak. "The car keys."

"Miss McCoy, I'm not supposed to –"

"Give. Me. The. Keys." I say. I stare him straight in the eye and he takes a step back before nodding his head once. He pulls out his car keys and drops them in my hand. I head off toward the front door when he clears his throat.

"Are you..." he pauses. "Should you get dressed?"

"Who the fuck am I trying to impress?" I ask. His eyes widen for a moment and a wave of understanding washes over him. He nods his head and I turn toward the black sedan parked in front of the house.

This has gone far enough.

39

DOMINIC

I THOUGHT I'd go straight to Tim McCoy from Aiden's last night, but when I drove into town my resolve wavered. Now I'm drinking my third cup of coffee as I stare at the stack of letters.

What if he doesn't believe me?

What if he already knows?

What if he *forgives* her?

The more I think about this, the less certain I am. The more it seems like I'm destined to fail. What am I trying to do, anyway? I have to convince Tim to turn against his wife, and somehow figure out what's going on with Mara. *Then*, if I'm able to do all that, I have to get Mara back.

What if she doesn't want to come back?

I shake my head and pull out my phone again. I read her text over and over until I'm sure she's there against her will.

She doesn't want to be there. I know her. I saw it in her eyes when she left. I saw it in the way she recoiled when Vincent touched her. I can see it in her text.

This isn't her choice.

I push my mug aside and stand up. I tuck the stack of letters under my arm and stalk out the front door. I swing myself into the cab of my truck and start the engine, peeling down the driveway toward Main Street. I can hardly hear the sound of the engine over the beating of my heart. I'm staring through a tunnel, and all I can see is the McCoy hotel at the end of the road. I glance at the passenger seat at the letters, and I try to think of what I'm going to say.

Mr. McCoy, I...

Tim, I have something to tell you.

Tim, is there somewhere we can talk?

My breath is shallow and my vision is blurry around the edges. I pull up outside the hotel and jump out of the truck, grabbing the papers and tucking them under my arm once again. I walk up the pathway toward the hotel's main entrance and push the door open.

I breathe a sigh of relief when no one is at the front desk. My eyes scan the room, and I wonder where Tim McCoy could be. I turn down the hallway toward the office where we spoke.

My hand is trembling when I lift it to knock on the door. With one more deep breath, I rap my knuckles against the wooden panels of the door and wait for a response. I look up and down the hallway, praying that Margaret McCoy doesn't appear around the corner.

I knock again.

Nothing.

My shoulders slump, and I turn away from the door when a voice calls out behind me.

"Can I help you with anything?"

I turn to see one of the housekeepers. I know her. We went to school together. I know pretty much everyone in this town.

"Katie!" I call out, trying to sound casual. "I'm looking for Tim McCoy."

"Huh," she replies with a smile and a frown. "Okay."

She smiles at me and motions down toward the lobby. "He

and Mrs. McCoy are having their breakfast in the dining room. I can show you the way."

"No!" Her eyebrows jump up and I take a deep breath. I try to control my voice. "I can't..." I pause, looking at Katie. "Can you get him for me? It has to be him. *Only* him."

She frowns slightly but nods her head. "Are you okay, Dominic?"

"I'm fine. Please, Katie. Can you get him for me?"

She stares at me for a few moments and then nods her head. "Wait in here," she says, pulling out a key ring and opening the office door. "I'll be back."

"Thank you," I tell her. She looks at me for a long moment and after a pause, her lips curl up into a smile.

"You and Mara seem really happy together. I'm rooting for you."

I open my mouth and close it again. I shake my head. "What are you talking about?"

She laughs. "Come on, Dominic. It's a small town. Everyone knows. You guys seemed really happy, and I hope it works out. I saw her when she was leaving."

"Do you know what happened?"

She shakes her head. "Not really. I overheard Margaret threatening her with something, but I couldn't make out what it was." She looks at me and smiles. "I'll get Tim. Wait here."

She closes the door gently and I slump into a chair, laying the stack of letters on my lap and putting my head in my hands.

The whole town knows??

I sigh and shake my head. Of course they do. Who were we kidding? Ethan could tell I was attracted to her the very first time I saw her at Harold's bar. I remember the way my arm felt when she touched it, and the way every look she gave me sent a thrill down through my stomach. I close my eyes and think of that smile of hers.

I'm lost in my thoughts when the door opens. I jump up and catch the stack of letters as they start to fall off my lap.

"Dominic!" Tim says in a hushed voice as he closes the office door. "What's all this about?"

Suddenly, I'm at a loss for words. I look at this man and see kindness in his eyes, and I hesitate. Do I really want to ruin his marriage?

He doesn't give me a chance to change my mind. His eyes shift to the stack of letters and he frowns.

"What are those? Is that... is that Margaret's handwriting?"

I glance at the stack of letters and take a deep breath.

"Tim, I... Mr. McCoy," I start, my voice catching in my throat. "I'm sorry to be the one to tell you this..."

"Spit it out, son," he says. His upper lip is trembling and the sides of his forehead are starting to get red. I feel the tension in his body from where I sit.

I stand up and show him the stack of letters. "Aiden found these when he was cleaning out the attic at our old house," I explain. "They're... They're addressed to my father. From Margaret."

Tim's mouth opens as he looks at the letters. "There are dozens of them!"

I nod. "I'm sorry, Tim."

I take the top letter off the stack and hand it to him. "This was the last letter. I think..." I pause again, swallowing. "My brothers and I think that it was the reason that Margaret took such a... uh... *disliking* to us."

Tim McCoy grabs the letter and opens it up. The blood drains from his face as he reads through the letter, and then he slumps down into a chair. He puts his head in his hand and shakes his head.

"This..." His voice trails off and he looks at the paper again. "I've been faithful all these years, and..."

"I had no idea," I say, sitting down across from him. "None of us did."

He looks up at me, his eyes suddenly clear. "So her insistence on buying the trucking business... Her ridiculous hatred of you and your brothers... All if it...?"

I shrug. "It looks like it was because of this," I say, motioning to the letter. "Because my father broke it off. I don't know how it's related to Mara, but I can't help but think..." My voice trails off and I struggle to find the words to express myself.

He shakes his head over and over until a lump forms in my throat. I shouldn't have done this. His face scrunches up and he keeps shaking his head back and forth, back and forth. I watch him slowly crumble in front of me until tears start streaming from his eyes. A pain goes through my chest as I watch him.

I shouldn't have done this. I should have found another way.

We both jump when the door opens. Margaret appears in the doorway. Tim stands up. He pulls his shoulders back and stares at her with fire in his eyes.

"You heartless bitch," he growls. I tense, staying immobile in my chair.

Margaret's eyes swing from him, to me, to the letters. She goes pale, grabbing the door jamb for support before her eyes go dark and her mouth purses into a thin line.

"So now you know," she snarls. "Well, it only took you ten years to put it together."

"What else have you lied about? Why did Mara leave?"

"Oh, grow up," she spits. "You should be thanking me for providing you with all this," she says, sweeping her arm in a wide circle. "Without me you'd be broke and alone."

"Where is my daughter," Tim growls.

"She's where she belongs, with her fiancé." Her black eyes swing to me, and her lip curls into a snarl. "I'd rather die than let her date a Clarke."

I stand up. Despite herself, she takes a step backward. She looks so tiny next to my huge, six-foot-four frame, but she squares her shoulders.

"Where is she," I growl. Her face relaxes and she smiles. A shiver passes down my spine.

"I told you: she's with her fiancé. I gave her the choice: you, or him. She chose him."

"I don't believe you," I growl. I take another step toward her but this time Margaret stands her ground.

"Leave us," Tim says. I turn back to look at him, but his eyes are locked on his wife. He waves his hand at me. "Leave us," he repeats. "I'll be in touch."

Something in his voice leaves no space for argument. I glance at the two of them before stalking out the door without looking back.

40

———

MARA

MY KNUCKLES ARE white as I grip the steering wheel. My slippers are sliding on the pedals and it takes all my concentration to stay on the road. I can't think of anything except the burning anger in the pit of my stomach.

I've never been this angry. It's almost like an out-of-body experience. All I can do is ride the wave of fury as I drive down the road. My vision is glued on the pavement in front of me. The car is powerful, and every time my foot sinks on the pedal, it accelerates forward. I breathe in and out through my nose as I press the accelerator down a fraction further.

My mother and Vincent used me. They used me to get my father to sign an agreement passing on the business to me and my future husband. They promised to take care of Dominic, but they lied.

The pain of that lie is like a dagger in the back. I could live with my guilt. I could tell myself that I was making up for the accident ten years ago, and I was giving Dominic another chance at a good life. I could have watched from a distance as he moved on from me, and used the rest of my life as a chance to atone.

184

If Dominic had been able to have a good life, it would have been worth it.

But now, all of that is gone. I've got nothing. I've lost the man that I love, I've lost my trust in my family, and I'm engaged to a man that I despise. The only reason I had to stay with him is gone.

I've got nothing.

Nothing, except black anger in my heart and a taste for blood in my mouth.

I turn onto the highway toward the city center where Vincent works. I see the tall buildings in the distance and my heart fills with fury.

I hate his slicked-back hair. I hate his perfectly tailored suits. I hate his gaudy house, and his expensive tastes. I hate the fountain in the front yard, and the wide marble steps. I hate his greed, and his heartlessness.

I see him for what he is now. He's a mercenary. He preyed on me, he preyed on my mother and father, and now it's gone too far. I won't let him prey on Dominic and his brothers too.

I grip the steering wheel a little bit harder as I press my foot down on the accelerator. My slipper starts to slide off the pedal and I adjust my foot, pressing it down a bit harder. The black sedan responds, and soon I'm racing down the freeway toward Vincent.

I don't even know what I'm going to say. I'll tell him I know. I'll tell Vincent that I'm telling my father about it all – that he'll never agree to anything. I'll tell him the deal is off.

It might make me look like a crazy person. They'll talk about me for months. I'll be the crazy ex-fiancée who showed up in her pajamas and started screaming in the office, but I don't care.

All I care about is Dominic. I tried to protect him but once again all I've done is hurt him. I can't let that happen again.

My foot presses down a little bit harder but this time the

slipper slides off. I try to get my foot back up, but my slipper jams itself under the brake pedal.

I'm going too fast.

The car swerves and I try to regain control. My heart jumps in my chest and my eyes widen as I feel the car slip out of my control. I try to grip the steering wheel and mash the pedals, but the back is fishtailing behind me.

I can't brake. The back of the car is spinning around out of control.

Maybe I scream, or maybe I'm stuck in silent shock. I can't be sure. My heart is thumping and my body is rigid as the car spins.

What they say in the movies is true: everything does slow down when you're about to die. I can see a pickup truck's shiny chrome grille coming straight toward my windshield. The driver's honking his horn, but it sounds elongated and far-away to my ears.

My whole body goes limp as I watch the front of my car crumple in a split-second that lasts an eternity. Soon, everything will be over.

I close my eyes and wait for it to end, and all I see is Dominic.

I melt into my seat. I think of the man I love as the truck crashes into me, and my world goes dark.

41

———

DOMINIC

I THROW a few clothes into a bag and toss it into my truck. I'll book a flight at the airport. I can't wait for Tim and Margaret to work things out. I have to see Mara *now*.

I haven't heard from her since that text, and Margaret's reaction convinced me that something else is going on. She's holding something over Mara's head, and I need to find out what that thing is.

I need to see her. I need to hear it from her lips that she's choosing Vincent over me.

If she isn't, then I want to wrap my arms around her and cover her in kisses. I never want to let her go again.

As I drive down the highway, I turn off the radio and try to make sense of my thoughts. Mara *told* me that her parents used her in the business deal for the hotel that burned down. What's stopping them from doing it again?

But the thing is, in order for her to go back to Vincent, she'd have to be forced.

They'd have to be threatening her with something – even Katie said so. What could they possibly threaten her with? What

187

would be so important that she would leave everything behind, including *me*?

My head hurts as I try to figure it out. I take long, deep breaths as I make the three-hour drive to the nearest airport.

I know she wants to be with me. I cling on to that text for dear life.

"*I wish I could.*"

She *wants* to be with me.

The sun is going down, and I drive in silence. I'm not even sure where Mara lives. I don't even know if there are flights tonight. All I know is that I'm going to the airport, and nothing can stop me.

My phone rings and I see Tim McCoy's name pop up. I hit answer and put him on speakerphone.

"Tim, I need Mara's address. I'm going to California."

"I... What?"

"Text me her address."

"Dominic... Okay. I'll send it over."

"Do you know what's going on?"

"They threatened her," he says in a low voice. I nod as I drive down the highway. "Dominic," he continues, "They threatened to put your business on the blacklist. That's why she agreed to go with Vincent."

"What? What do you mean?" I ask. My heart drops to my stomach and I struggle to understand what he's talking about. I hear Tim McCoy take a deep breath.

"They needed my approval to pass the business on to her and her husband. That arrogant ass, Vincent." I can hear the venom in his voice as he says Vincent's name. "So they told her they'd drag your name through the mud."

My heart starts thumping. I try to speak but my voice barely comes out "And she agreed?"

"She did," Tim says. "Dominic, she loves you, you know."

I try to answer, but I can't. I nod my head as if he can see me, and finally he speaks again.

"I'll send you that address." He sighs. "Thank you."

"No, thank you, Tim," I finally manage to say. The phone clicks and I put it down on the passenger seat. I grip the steering wheel and blink my eyes until they clear.

She loves me.

She did this for me?

I can hardly believe it. She'd put herself in that position... she would actually *marry* a man that doesn't love her, and give him the family business? She would do that just so I would be able to continue making furniture?

I feel grateful and ashamed at the same time. I don't deserve this. My ears are burning and my heart is thumping as I try to keep my eyes focused on the road.

My phone buzzes and I see Tim's name pop up with an address. I glance at it and take a deep breath.

I'm coming, Mara.

THE REST of the drive seems to take an eternity. After a few more miles, I turn on the radio to try to drown out my thoughts. I've never been surer of any decision. I know I need to go and see her.

I think of Vincent's weasel face and the anger starts to flood my veins. *If he happens to get punched in the nose, then so be it.*

When I get to the airport, it's late at night. I walk up to the counter and take a deep breath.

"I need a flight to San Francisco," I tell the lady behind the desk. She looks at me and raises her eyebrows before tapping on her computer.

"I'm sorry sir. There aren't any flights until tomorrow morning. The earliest I can get you there is 8:00am, San Fran time."

"That's fine. Here's my card," I say as I hand her my credit card. She nods as if this is the most normal thing in the world. Within a few minutes, she's printing my ticket.

"Can I book a car from here as well?" I ask.

"The counter over there will be able to help you," she says as she hands me a boarding pass. I nod in thanks and take the ticket, walking over to the desk.

Once everything is organized, I check the time. I have five and a half hours before the flight leaves, so I might as well try to get some sleep. I find a row of seats and lay down, trying to fit my huge body on the tiny chairs. It only takes a few minutes for the sleep to make my eyelids heavy. In a few hours, I'll be seeing Mara in person and I can tell her everything that I want to tell her.

I'll tell her I love her.

I'll tell her to come back to me.

I'll tell her I don't care about the business, that all I want is her.

I'll tell her everything in my heart and I'll never let her go.

When I drift off to sleep in the airport waiting lounge, I can hear her laugh. I can smell her perfume and I can see her smile painted on my eyelids. My heart slows down and I finally feel like things will be okay.

42

DOMINIC

THE FLIGHT IS UNEVENTFUL. It takes just over four hours, but it feels like an eternity. My whole body is aching from the uncomfortable sleep and the tiny airplane seats, and I feel like I've aged ten years overnight. As the wheels touch down, I look out the window and a wave of nervousness washes over me.

I've never done anything like this.

When I file off the plane with my carry-on bag, the nervousness fades away. By the time I'm getting into the rental car, I'm focused and ready.

As I drive toward Mara's address, my heart starts to beat a little bit faster. It's not the angry, outraged heartbeat that I had yesterday. It feels like it's beating *for* her – like the only reason for me to be here is to tell her everything that's in my heart.

The GPS in the rental car guides me until the houses get bigger and the gates get higher. I frown as I look at these mansions, stuck together with no room to breathe. My cabin back home is one tenth of the size of these places, but I have all of the Adirondacks as my backyard.

I wouldn't trade that for anything.

The voice on the GPS tells me that my destination is on the

right, and I look at the tall black wrought-iron gate leading up to a big house. I pull up to the gate and press the buzzer.

"Yes?" Says a voice on the other side.

"I'm here to see Mara McCoy," I say.

There's a pause, and then the voice comes back. "She's not here right now."

"Where is she?" I answer. My eyebrows knit together and I check the address. It's definitely the right house, but where else would she be? It's not even ten o'clock yet.

The voice doesn't answer. Instead, the black gate swings open and I drive through.

I try not to let the intimidation overwhelm me as I drive up to the house. Did Mara do this for me? Or did she really want to live here? It's huge and luxurious, and she'd obviously be living a life of wealth that I'd never be able to provide for her.

I shake my head and ignore those niggling thoughts. I stop the car in front of the wide front steps. As I get out, the front door opens and a man appears. It's not Vincent, and he's wearing a crisp white jacket with black pants.

"I'm William," he says. "You're here to see Miss McCoy? Is she expecting you?"

"I, uh... No," I answer. I suddenly feel foolish. I'm wearing a flannel plaid shirt and old jeans, and I haven't shaved my beard in days. I don't belong here.

William nods to me and motions for me to come in. I climb the steps and swallow as I cross the threshold and enter the huge house. He leads me to a room off to the side and I sit down on an expensive-looking leather chair.

"Would you like something to drink?"

"I'm fine," I snap. "Where's Mara?"

William chews his lip and glances out the window. "I... I'm not sure, sir."

I frown. "You're not sure? What do you mean, 'you're not sure'?"

"If you leave your name, I can tell either Miss McCoy or Mr. –"

"How long has she been gone?"

"Since yesterday," he answers.

My eyes widen and my heart drops to my stomach. I pull out my phone and dial her number. It goes straight to voicemail and I look at William. "Where the fuck is she?"

Something is wrong. I can feel it. I can tell by the way William is staring at the ground and shifting his weight from foot to foot.

"Tell me goddamn it! Where is she?"

"She left yesterday morning. She seemed... upset."

I take a step toward him. My mouth is dry and my heart is beating hard. "Tell me where she is," I say in a low voice.

Suddenly William looks scared. He shakes his head. "I don't know," he whispers. "She took the car."

My phone rings and I rush to pick it up. It's Tim McCoy, and when I answer I already know something is wrong.

"Dominic," he says, breathless. "Are you in California?"

"I can't find her, Tim. She's not at home and they don't know where she is."

"There's been an accident," he says as his voice cracks. "She's in the hospital."

"What!" I yell, glancing at William.

"They just identified her and called me as her emergency contact. I'll send you the hospital name."

"I'm on my way."

I brush past William and rush out the door. I plug the address that Tim sends into the GPS and rush to turn on the engine. My tires squeal as I accelerate back down the driveway. I curse as the gate swings open all too slowly, and finally turn off and leave that awful mansion behind me.

My mouth is dry. My knuckles are white as I grip the steering wheel. My heart is thumping and all I can hear is Tim's voice.

There's been an accident.

I should never have let her go. If she hadn't come here – if she'd have just *talked* to me, or talked to her father – this wouldn't have happened. If I hadn't spent the evening smashing up that nightstand and drinking myself to sleep, I could have found her and spoken to her.

I drive as fast as I can along the blue line on the GPS until I get to the hospital. I rush to Reception and ask for her. I'm led along winding hallways until I cross swinging doors with three awful words above them: Intensive Care Unit.

She's in the ICU. My heart drops and I try to hold back my panic. It's not until I see her lying in the hospital bed that I let myself sob. There are tubes sticking out of her mouth, her arms, her stomach. She's got bandages on her head and her leg is in a cast. There are machines beeping and nurses milling around.

Her eyes are closed, and I grab her hand as I sit in yet another uncomfortable chair. I put my forehead down on her hand and let the tears flow from my eyes. They soak the blue blanket on the hospital bed and I just sit there and sob until my eyes run dry.

A nurse puts her hand on my shoulder and I look up through tear-filled eyes.

"Is she going to be okay?" I manage to say.

The nurse swallows and her lips purse into a thin line. "She's in critical condition," she answers. "We'll know more in a few hours."

"Please," I beg. "Please, just tell me she'll be okay."

The nurse nods. "We're doing everything we can." She squeezes my shoulder and I turn back to Mara, stroking her hand and letting the tears fall from my eyes.

43

MARA

I WAKE up to the sound of heated voices.

"She's my fiancée! Get this man out of here!"

"Sir, please calm down."

"He has no right to be here!"

I frown as I try to understand why that voice is bothering me. I try to remember who it belongs to, and why I don't want to hear it. I try to open my eyes, but I can't get them to open. It's like my body doesn't belong to me anymore. I hear that voice again and it sends fear radiating through my chest.

"Get him out of here!"

"Sir, please calm down, or we'll have to remove both of you."

"She never wanted to be with you, you bastard," another voice says. My heart starts beating faster and I pray that he'll say something else. I want to hear that voice again. That's the voice I want to listen to.

"You used her. You have no right to be here."

"I have *every* right to be here! You should be holed up in the mountains, back where you belong."

"Fuck you," the voice says again. "I love her more than you could love anyone... or any*thing*."

My eyes fly open and I take a deep breath in. "Dominic!" I call out. I struggle to focus my eyes and the voices stop. Someone takes my hand and the voice is next to me now.

"I'm here, baby, I'm here. I'm right here."

I look at the shape beside me and blink a few times until my vision clears.

It's him!

"Dominic," I breathe. He's staring at me with his eyebrows drawn together, stroking my arm and holding my hand as he crouches next to me.

"I'm here." He kisses my hand and then brings his lips to my forehead. "I'm here."

I breathe in that familiar smell and close my eyes again. "Dominic," I breathe.

"You were in an accident," he says softly. "You're in the hospital. You're safe now."

I don't understand what he means, and I don't understand what's going on. All I know is he's here, he's holding my hand and kissing my forehead. He's brushing the hair off my face and whispering to me. I can feel him and smell him and see him.

He's here.

I take deep breaths as I try to make sense of what's going on.

"Mara, darling," the other man says. I frown, turning toward him. It's Vincent. He's wearing a three-piece suit, and he looks stiff and uncomfortable. I shake my head and look back at Dominic, trying to keep my breath steady and my eyes on him.

"Mara, look at me," Vincent says.

"Go away," I croak. My throat hurts and it's hard to speak. It barely comes out above a hoarse whisper. "Get out."

A nurse appears and puts her hand on Vincent's shoulder. He brushes her off and stares at me with fire in his eyes.

"I'm your fiancé!" He says. "Don't tell me to leave!"

"It's over," I croak. His face contorts into a snarl and he spins around, brushing the nurse's arm away. He stomps out of the room and I let out a deep breath. I close my eyes and squeeze Dominic's hand. I focus on the soft stroking of his hand over mine, and the gentle sound of his voice until I drift off to sleep again.

WHEN I WAKE UP AGAIN, Dominic is curled up into a chair that's much too small for him, snoring lightly as he sleeps. I watch him for a few moments and a smile drifts over my face. As if he can sense my stare, he wakes up and immediately leans forward.

"Mara! You're awake!"

"Yeah," I croak. My voice still sounds like a toad.

Dominic smiles and tears start to fill his eyes. "I've been so worried about you," he whispers, leaning down to kiss my hand. He strokes my cheek and shakes his head. "So worried."

"What are you doing here?"

"I came to tell you that you didn't have to do this. I found out about the deal you made with your mother and Vincent. Mara, you don't need to protect me. I'll be fine. Don't ruin your life for me."

I try to smile and it feels like my lips are cracking. Dominic puts his forehead against mine and kisses me.

"I love you, Mara."

Even though my whole body is aching, and I can't move or speak or breathe without something hurting, his words make me feel like I'm floating. I smile, ignoring my cracked lips and let the tears flow from my eyes.

"I love you too, Dominic."

"Come back with me," he whispers. "Be with me."

"I will," I answer. My heart beats a little bit faster, and the machines around me beep along with it. Dominic squeezes my hand and kisses my lips. For the first time since I left Lang Creek, I feel at peace.

A knock on the door interrupts us, and my father pokes his head through. Concern lines his face and he rushes to my side.

"Mara," he breathes. "My God. I came as soon as I could."

"I'm fine, Dad." I lie. "Thank you for coming."

He holds my other hand and I close my eyes, feeling the love of my father and Dominic radiate through me. I open my eyes again and turn to my father.

"Where's Mom?"

My dad looks away from me and glances at Dominic. He shakes his head.

"Don't worry about that," he says. "Just focus on getting better."

I frown, trying to understand him. "What do you mean? Where is she?"

"We can talk about this later, Mara. You need to heal."

"Dad," I say a little bit louder. "Tell me what's going on. I've been kept in the dark my whole life."

My dad looks at Dominic and takes a deep breath. "I confronted your mother after Dominic spoke to me," he says slowly. "She admitted what she was doing with you and Vincent. I told her I'd never pass the business on to you if you married Vincent. I told her I'd give it to Dominic, instead."

"What?" Dominic interrupts. My dad shakes his head.

"It's true. I'd rather you have it." He pauses. "She left, Mara. I don't know where she is. She drained our accounts and took the insurance payout, and she left in the middle of the night. I found out about your accident a few hours later, and I came as soon as I could."

I stare at my father for a few moments and then close my eyes. My heart is breaking, and a tear rolls down my cheek.

She left?

Do we mean nothing to her? She just took our money and ran?

As if he can sense my pain, Dominic squeezes my hand.

"Mara, we'll figure it out," he says in a low voice. I open my eyes to look at the love of my life and nod my chin down. "You hear me?" he continues. "We'll figure it out. Just get yourself better and come home with us."

"Home," I croak as I try to smile. "That sounds nice."

Dominic leans over and places a soft kiss on my lips. "I love you, Mara McCoy."

"And I love you, Dominic Clarke."

EPILOGUE
DOMINIC

IT TAKES a couple weeks for Mara to get strong enough to fly, but I don't mind. Tim and I take turns at the hospital, and otherwise I explore the nearby area.

Southern California is nice, but it's not home. I miss the lush pine trees and jagged peaks. I gaze over the Pacific Ocean and take in the rolling hills, and I sigh. I turn away from the ocean and get back in the rental car, heading toward the hospital.

Tim and Mara are waiting for me at the entrance.

"Wheelchair!" I exclaim as I get out of the car.

Mara rolls her eyes. "They made me take it. I don't need it," she says.

I put my arm under her shoulders and help her up. I see her wince as we move and a pain passes through my heart. The wheelchair seems like a good idea to me. Tim nods to me and jumps into the driver's seat as I get in the back of the car with Mara.

She rests her head against my shoulder and her eyelids close. I watch her chest rise and fall, and my own chest squeezes when I see how small she is. She's lost so much weight in the hospital, and her cheeks look almost sunken in. She looks so weak. My heart starts beating and I worry that it's too soon – that we shouldn't be moving her yet. It's a long way to Lang Creek. We have a five hour flight and then a three hour drive before we get home. It'll be a full day of traveling.

"Are you sure you're okay?" I whisper to her.

"Shh," she says as she pats my leg. "I just want to go home."

I WATCH her like a hawk until I'm laying her down in her bed at the back of the hotel. Mara's face is worn and she looks at me through sleepy eyes.

"Don't go," she whispers to me. "I want to wake up with you here."

I manage a smile and nod. I kick off my shoes and lie next to her, feeling her frail body drift off to sleep next to me. I hold her close, stroking her arm up and down until sleep takes me too.

THE NEXT FEW weeks are rough. Mara is weak, and I worry that she should be under someone's care. She should have a nurse here, and she shouldn't be moving as much as she is. I can see her stubbornness though, in the way that she swings her legs over the side of the bed every day, and forces herself to walk up and down Main Street until she looks exhausted. She grits her teeth and tries to hide her pain, but I see it when she thinks I'm not looking. I sleep next to her every night, and wake up next to her every morning.

On one chilly autumn afternoon, I load up the last of the headboards into my truck and drive over to the McCoy Hotel.

Mara is waiting for me outside, wearing a big grin on her face. She still has a boot on from the knee down, but she can walk almost normally. Her scars are fading, and she gives me a big wave as I pull up to the hotel.

"Congratulations, Mr. Clarke," she calls out to me. "That's the last of the furniture for the hotel! A few finishing touches and the renovations will be complete!"

"Better late than never," I respond as I jump out of the cab and smile to her. She wraps her arms around my neck and plants a big kiss on my lips. I pull away and drag my fingers through her hair, inhaling her sweet perfume and getting lost in her eyes.

"You're so beautiful, Mara."

Her eyes crinkle as she smiles and she sticks her tongue out. "Even now?"

"Even now," I reply with a grin. I rub my nose against hers and she laughs.

Tim appears behind her and he nods to me. "Looks great, Dominic. Thank you for your work."

"No problem at all," I reply, helping him unload the last headboard. We carry it upstairs as Mara follows us. I take a step back and sigh in satisfaction once it's installed. Mara slips her hand around my waist and leans her head against my shoulder. I squeeze her against me and she smiles. She looks over to her dad.

"See, Dad, we don't need Mom here. The hotel looks better than ever before. We're already doing 15% better than we were last year at this point in the season!"

Tim smiles sadly. He puts his arm around his daughter and kisses her temple. "I'm just glad you're okay," he replies. I can see the pain in his eyes whenever Margaret is mentioned. Since she left, we haven't heard a word from her. She disappeared with the insurance money, and she hasn't been back since. She took all their savings, and I had to finish out the contract without being paid.

Sometimes, Tim stares out through a window and I know he's thinking of her. It makes my chest ache for him. She took more than just money when she left. She took something from Tim, too.

Tim shakes his head and puts a smile on his face. Mara pulls away from her dad and nudges him. Tim smiles and pulls something out of his breast pocket. He hands it to me.

I frown, looking down at the paper. I unfold it and shake my head.

"For your work," Tim says. "I know we couldn't pay you, and I appreciate you finishing the job. You're a good man, Dominic."

"Tim, I can't accept this," I say, staring at the agreement for part ownership of the McCoy Hotel. "It's way too much. You can pay me the rest when you have the money," I answer, handing him the papers.

Mara smiles and shakes her head. "I told you he wouldn't accept," she answers with a laugh. "Come on, Dominic. It'll be yours eventually anyways."

I glance at her frown. "What are you talking about?"

She laughs. "When we get married and live happily ever after!" she says. I look from her to Tim and a smile spreads across my face.

"Are you proposing to me? In front of your dad?"

"I'd propose in front of the whole world," she says, wrapping her arms around my waist. "You're mine, and I'm yours. Everything I have is yours too – including this place. You've put enough work into it to own part of it."

My throat tightens and my eyes start to prickle. I try to swallow as I pull her in tighter to me. Tim smiles at me and nods his head.

"Welcome to the family, Dominic. I never thought I'd say those words," he adds with a chuckle.

"I never thought I'd hear them," I answer. Mara lifts her chin up and wraps her arms around me a little bit tighter. I dip my lips down to hers and taste that sweet kiss one more time.

You're mine, and I'm yours.

Mara's voice rings in my ears. I never thought I'd hear *those* words, either, and I never thought they'd sound so good.

~

Grab your own exclusive bonus chapter:
https://www.lilianmonroe.com/subscribe

Psst... Keep reading for your preview of Book 3!

RUN TO ME

THE CLARKE BROTHERS SERIES: BOOK 3

1

ZOE

"GOOD LUCK TOMORROW, MONKEY." My heart squeezes and my hand tightens around my cell phone. I know that there's no way I can make it to my daughter's piano recital, but it still makes me feel like a bad mother to miss it. I'm glad she can't see the tears in my eyes right now.

"I'm not a monkey, Mom," Audrey answers with a sigh. "And I'm not small. Could a monkey play piano?"

"Not as well as you," I smile. "Alright come on, put your grandmother back on the phone."

"Grandma!" Audrey yells straight into the receiver. I pull the phone away from my ear and cringe as she yells. I listen as their phone exchanges hands and smile when I hear Audrey humming in the background.

"You'll record her recital for me?" I ask when my mother comes on the phone. My voice is trembling, and I swallow to keep it steady.

"Every minute of it, Zoe. Don't worry."

"I'm not worried. Just... disappointed. This will be the longest I've been away from her since she was born."

"Don't torture yourself," my mother says. I can almost see her pursing her lips and shaking her head. "You daughter will be fine. She'll be great, actually. You'll realize she doesn't need you at all, and it'll make you feel happy and heartbroken at the same time. Take it from someone who knows," she adds ruefully. "Just finish this job and come back. This contract will be sorted out in no time, and everything will be back to normal."

As much as I want to fight it, my mother's platitudes help. Her words are comforting and my shoulders start to relax. I nod.

As if she can see me nod from the other end of the phone, my mom speaks again. This time her voice is soft, and it sounds like a warm hug.

"And Zoe?" She asks, letting my name hang in the air.

I clear my throat. "Yeah, Mom?"

"Try and enjoy yourself. You're a beautiful, successful single woman. You have some time for yourself now, for the first time since Mark passed. Make the most of it. We'll be fine. Won't we, Audrey?" She adds, slightly louder. I hear Audrey giggle in the background.

"Of course!" Comes my daughter's voice in the distance

I smile. "Give her a big hug for me, okay?"

"I will. Now go. Go to the town bar, have a drink, and relax. I'm your mother and I still get to tell you what to do once in a while."

I chuckle and take a deep breath. "Sounds like something I can manage."

"Good. I love you, Zoe. This will all be over soon. Don't worry about a thing."

My throat tightens and I nod my head. When I speak, my voice is barely a whisper. "I love you too, Mom. Thank you."

"Don't mention it. Now go and get yourself a drink!"

I laugh and we hang up the call. I'm sitting on the edge of my hard hotel bed without moving. I stare at my phone's blank screen and take a deep breath.

She's right. It's only a couple months, and I already know that Audrey will be fine. If anything, it's me who will suffer from the separation the most. She's busy with school and soccer and piano, with her friends and with her grandmother. She'll hardly think about me at all.

Now me, on the other hand... That's a different story. When Audrey's father, my husband, died of cancer when she was two, I felt like my heart would never recover. I still don't know if it has, and it's been just over six years. It's been alright to be alone, because I've had her. Now she's on the other side of the country and I'm kind of freaking out.

For the hundredth time since I got to my hotel, I look at the dingy room and sigh. I try not to breathe too deeply, because the air in the room is stuffy and smells vaguely of mildew. I get up as the bedsprings squeak, avoiding my reflection in the mirror hanging on the wall. I don't want to be reminded of how old and tired I surely look. Being a single mother with an active job will do that to a person.

I run my fingers over the file on the desk: my assignment. Or rather, my punishment, as I've come to see it. I knew that working for a bureaucratic entity like the government could be difficult, but I never imagined I'd get relegated to the middle of nowhere for trying to show initiative. Now I have to implement my forest fire management systems in a National Park on the opposite side of the country.

I should probably be flattered. It's supposed to be an honor to be sent here, since governments are usually so slow to implement new programs. But the fire that happened here in Lang Creek last year shook the entire Parks community, and my boss volunteered me up as a tribute. Or 'gave me the opportunity of a lifetime,' as he described it.

I sigh, shaking my head. Maybe my mom is right. I just need to relax. Tomorrow I drive down to the shitty little town that I've been assigned to, and I'll deal with it then. For now I just need to empty my mind and relax. If I go to the bar and grab a drink, maybe the aching loneliness inside me will go away just a little, and I won't be worried about what my daughter is doing every minute that I'm away from her.

I swear I've never been a helicopter mom, but being a couple thousand miles away from your only child will do that to a person.

I slip out the door and get in the elevator. I glance in the lobby bar and keep walking. It's dark and empty in there, with a dated decor and a slight sense of melancholy. Not what I need right now.

I'm not sure what I do need, but I head down the road towards the strip of shops and bars that I saw on the drive in. Calling it 'downtown' is a bit generous. Soon, I can hear music and people as I round the corner. I turn into the first bar I see.

It's loud, and dark, and full of people. It's exactly what I wanted. I slip through the crowd and find an empty stool at the end of the bar. It only takes a few moments before the bartender takes my order.

"Gin and soda, please," I say, and he nods. I let my eyes drift across the room and feel my lips curl upwards. Somehow, even when I'm a grown woman, my mother still knows exactly what I need. I need noise and people and laughter and distractions, so that all the thoughts in my head will be drowned out.

The bartender drops my drink in front of me and I take my first sip with my eyes closed. As soon as the liquid hits my tongue, my eyes fly open and I put the drink down. He must have emptied half the bottle in this glass. The gin tastes fruity and fresh with that indescribable tangy aftertaste. The bartender chuckles as I stare at my glass.

"Looked like you needed it," he grins. "First one's on me."

He's an older man with a huge salt-and-pepper beard. His eyes are dark, but kind. I nod.

"Thanks."

He grins and turns to another customer.

Maybe I do need it. I'm starting to regret not looking at myself in the mirror before leaving. If he can tell I'm stressed, I must look like a mess. I comb my fingers through my hair and wipe my fingers under my eyes, checking them for streaks of mascara. Seeing my fingers come back clean, I take a deep breath and take another sip.

My heartbeat slows down and my eyes relax. I lean my forearms on the bar and let my eyes drift across the room. Something is happening in the corner, like there's a hum of excitement surrounding something.

I turn and see a band starting to set up on a tiny stage. It's more like a step, with barely enough room for the two men to work alongside each other. I lean against the bar, sipping my drink and watching them set up. There are two men setting up the drums and microphones, taking guitars out and testing the sound. The bartender appears beside me and I nod to the band.

"Who are they?"

"Them?" He asks, nodding to the band. "They're the Mad Hatters," he replies. "Play here every second Saturday of the month. Bring the house down every time."

I grunt in acknowledgement and turn back to the band. 'Bringing the house down' must have a different meaning here than in the big city. There's someone new on the step, or the stage, or whatever you'd call it. He's got his back to me, but something in the way he moves makes my heart jump. He's standing tall, and his black tee-shirt is stretched across his broad back. I can see the outline of his muscles through the thin fabric. He leans over to pull a cable towards the front, and his shirt lifts up to show the waistband of his underwear.

A blush stains my cheeks.

Why am I blushing? My eyes widen as he turns towards the front, tapping on the microphone and smiling. My heart jumps as I hear his voice over the speakers. It's smooth and deep, and his smile makes a couple girls in the crowd yelp.

"How's everyone doing tonight?"

It's lame and stereotypical. It's what every rock star and wannabe rock star would say, but it still makes the heat rush towards my thighs. He smiles again and slings his guitar over his shoulder, grabbing it and sliding his fingers over the strings. He strums it once and a few more people yell out.

Then, they play. They play and sing and shout and just as the barman said, they bring the house down. I sip my drink and watch as he sings the first song. I don't hear a word. I don't see anything except him, I don't hear anything except the sound of his voice.

2

ETHAN

I ALMOST STOP SINGING and mess up the whole song when she comes out on the dance floor. I catch myself in time, but it's a struggle to keep up. She's dancing like no one is watching, even though everybody in the room is staring at her. She's laughing, and finally, *finally,* she turns towards me.

When she looks at me, it takes all my self-control to keep playing. I'm glad we've rehearsed this song for hours, because at this point, playing the guitar is pure muscle memory. She stares at me and my blood turns to fire. Her lips curl upwards and I can feel myself getting hard.

By the time the first set it done, I have to know who she is. But by the time I put my guitar down she's already disappeared. My eyes scan the crowd and I frown.

Bethany Davis comes up to me, just like she does at every show, and flaps her eyelashes at me.

"Great set, Ethan," she says. She puts her hands on my forearm and presses her chest against me. "Your voice sounds better every week."

"Thanks, Beth," I reply. I take a step back and look over her shoulder. Beth presses her tits against me a bit more and says something that I don't hear. My breath catches in my throat.

There she is.

She's at the bar, in the corner. She's actually sitting in *my* seat. Didn't Carl tell her? He knows that I always sit there, and usually he saves the seat for me.

Not this time. This time, he's let this gorgeous brunette sit in my stool, and he's pouring her another drink. By the time I make it through the crowd to her, she's taking a sip. I watch her lips touch the edge of the glass and my cock pulses.

I clear my throat and tear my eyes away from her, turning to Carl.

"What's this? You're giving away my seat now?" I ask with a grin, glancing back at the woman before turning to Carl.

Carl chuckles. "Didn't think you'd mind," he replies, putting a beer down in front of me. I turn to the woman and let my eyes run up and down her body. I can hardly see straight. She's staring at me with a raised eyebrow and a smile playing in her eyes.

"This is your seat?" She asks. "Didn't see your name on it."

"It's sort of an unwritten rule," I answer, sliding into the stool next to hers.

She snorts and takes another sip. "You want me to move?" She asks, flashing a mischievous grin at me. My cock is pulsing between my legs and I smile back.

"Nah, you can stay," I answer. *I wouldn't want you to move for anything.* "So you're new in town?"

"Clearly," she answers. "Don't know all the rules yet."

"You'll learn."

She smiles again and shakes her head. "What if I don't like following rules?"

"That would be surprising."

"What, I look nice and innocent to you?"

"Something like that," I reply. "Maybe not innocent," I add. Another smile flashes across her face.

"No," she says slowly, running her finger around the edge of her glass. "Maybe not innocent."

I can't think straight. I know I have to play another set in a few minutes, but right now all I can think of is this woman and how badly I want to fuck her. She tucks a strand of hair behind her ear and I stare at the soft curve of her neck. My eyes drop down to her tits and back up to her face.

God, she's hot.

I clear my throat and shift in my seat, trying to think of something to say. My head is full of cotton and my cock is as hard as steel.

"You're a good dancer," I finally manage to say.

She laughs. "Thanks. You're a good singer."

I turn to her, not sure if she's joking or not. She smiles at me, and I know she isn't. She tilts her head and takes another sip of her drink. I do the same, putting my beer down at the same time as her.

"I'm Zoe," she says, reaching her hand over towards me.

"Ethan," I nod.

I take her hand in mine and ignore the pulsing between my legs. Her skin is soft and warm, and her hand feels like it fits perfectly in my palm. She grabs my hand firmly and shakes in once. Her eyes gleam and a smile stretches her lips as she finally pulls her hand away.

"Are you from here?" She asks, glancing around the bar.

I shake my head. "Nah, I'm from a town a couple hours away," I reply, not taking my eyes off her. "I just come up here to play."

She nods. "I was driving down from the airport and had to take a detour because of the rock slide on the freeway. So I guess you could say I was lucky, otherwise I never would have stopped here."

"You could say that," I reply with a grin. *You could say that I was the lucky one.* I clear my throat, looking away from her to keep my head from spinning. "I drove up to the rock slide this morning," I say, peeling the label off my beer. "It'll take them days to clear the road."

She nods, sipping her drink. "You guys get a lot of rockslides around here?"

I grunt. "Rockslides around here aren't usually that big. The odd one takes a day or two to clear. The end of spring, beginning of the summer is the worst for them, when the snow is melting and the rain is pouring down. Makes the rock faces weak." I glance up at her, seeing her eyes shoot up. "Don't worry, you're safe."

She laughs. "Good." We stare at each other for a moment until she clears her throat and takes another sip of her drink. She looks at me curiously.

"So why the Mad Hatters? Are you a big Lewis Carroll fan?" Her smile twitches.

"No, I just really like hats," I reply. She laughs, and my heart jumps. She shakes her head and throws me a look that makes my cock pulse again. "Nah," I add. "My mom used to read Alice in Wonderland to me when I was a kid. I loved that book, especially the scene with the Mad Hatter. I guess it just fit."

"Makes sense," she says.

"*If I had my own world, everything would be nonsense,*" I say almost automatically.

"*Nothing would be what it is, because everything would be what it isn't.*" Zoe answers. My eyes widen and a laugh tumbles out of me.

"*And contrary wise, what is, it wouldn't be.*"

"*And what it wouldn't be, it would. You see?*" She laughs as she says the last words and shakes her head.

I stare at her, slack-jawed. "I've never met anyone who can quote the Mad Hatter. Not even my own bandmates."

She blushes and stares at her drink. "I played the Mad Hatter in a school play when I was thirteen. It took me ages to learn those lines," she laughs. "I've never forgotten them. Didn't understand them then and still don't understand them now."

"I don't think you're supposed to understand them," I answer with a laugh. "So what are you doing here anyways? You don't sound like you're local."

She tilts her head to the side and hesitates. She licks her lips and I try not to stare at her, until finally she shrugs.

"Just passing through," she answers. I want to press her, but something in the way she says it makes me think she doesn't want me to ask. "I'm leaving again in the morning, need to go to my new job."

"That's a shame," I reply in a low growl. "It would have been nice to have more than one night together."

Her eyes flash and her grin twitches. "Who said we were having a night together?"

I open my mouth to answer when there's a tap on my shoulder. My drummer, Billy, is glancing from me to Zoe with an unimpressed look on his face.

"We're on. Unless you're too busy...?" He glances at Zoe, who blushes again. The color on her cheeks makes the desire coil in my stomach.

"You're a dickhead, Billy," I answer as he grins. I nod to the stage and start heading towards it when I turn around. I see Zoe slinging her bag over her shoulder and I frown.

"You're leaving?"

"I have an early morning tomorrow," she explains. We look at each other for a few moments and she leans against the bar. Impulsively, I take a step towards her, putting my hand on her waist and brushing my lips over her cheek. She trembles, and my cock pulses again.

"Don't leave before I'm done," I say softly into her ear. I pull away and watch as she wets her lips.

"Is that another rule of yours?" Zoe asks with an eyebrow raised.

"No."

"Okay... I'll stay," she says in a low voice. We stare at each other for a few moments and I finally tear myself away. I look for her when I get on stage and smile when I see her at the bar, sitting in my seat.

~

Keep reading **Run to Me**:
https://www.lilianmonroe.com/clarke-brothers-series

Sign up for my reader list to get bonus epilogues from all my books:
https://www.lilianmonroe.com/subscribe

ALSO BY LILIAN MONROE

For all books, visit:

www.lilianmonroe.com

Brother's Best Friend Romance

Shouldn't Want You

Can't Have You

Don't Need You

Won't Miss You

Military Romance

His Vow

His Oath

His Word

The Complete Protector Series

Enemies to Lovers Romance

Hate at First Sight

Loathe at First Sight

Despise at First Sight

The Complete Love/Hate Series

Secret Baby/Accidental Pregnancy Romance:

Knocked Up by the CEO

Knocked Up by the Single Dad

Knocked Up...Again!

Knocked Up by the Billionaire's Son

The Complete Unexpected Series

Yours for Christmas

Bad Prince

Heartless Prince

Cruel Prince

Broken Prince

Wicked Prince

Wrong Prince

Lone Prince

Fake Engagement/ Fake Marriage Romance:

Engaged to Mr. Right

Engaged to Mr. Wrong

Engaged to Mr. Perfect

Mr Right: The Complete Fake Engagement Series

Mountain Man Romance:

Lie to Me

Swear to Me

Run to Me

The Complete Clarke Brothers Series

Extra-Steamy Rock Star Romance:

Garrett

Maddox

Carter

The Complete Rock Hard Series

<u>Sexy Doctors:</u>

Doctor O

Doctor D

Doctor L

The Complete Doctor's Orders Series

<u>Time Travel Romance:</u>

The Cause

<u>A little something different:</u>

Second Chance: A Rockstar Romance in North Korea